Wichita Snatched

Wichita Detective
Book Seven

Patrick Andrews

ROUGH
EDGES
PRESS

Rough Edges Press
An Imprint of Wolfpack Publishing
9850 S. Maryland Parkway, Suite A-5 #323
Las Vegas, Nevada 89183

roughedgespress.com

Paperback ISBN 978-1-68549-299-1
eBook ISBN 978-1-68549-298-4
LCCN 2023939563

This novel is dedicated to my wonderful wife, Julie Christine.

WICHITA SNATCHED

CHAPTER 1

The new year of 1948 was a week old as Dwayne Wheeler, a slightly felonious private detective, and his wife Donna Sue arrived on a Monday morning at the downtown parking garage across from their office in the WKH Building.

Wordlessly, they got out of the vehicle and walked across the street. After an elevator ride up to the second floor, Dwayne unlocked the door, then stepped back to allow his wife to enter. She walked over to her desk and picked up the phone to call Millie at the Reliable Answering Service.

Dwayne waited for her to finish the call, and when she hung up, Donna Sue shrugged. "Nothing today."

"You know something, sweetie? I hope no capers pop up for a while."

"What do you want to do, Dwayne?"

"Let's go back to the apartment for a day or two of rest."

"Oh, come on! We've just had a whole weekend

there." She gave him a slightly flirtatious smile. "I'm all rested up, if you know what I mean."

Dwayne chuckled. "Boy, do I." He grew more serious as he went on, "Then how about we go to the Roadhouse Nightclub this evening?"

"Great idea," Donna Sue said. "We haven't seen Elmer Pettibone in a long time."

"That's right. We can find out how his taxi service is coming along."

"But if there aren't any cases for you to work on, I suppose it doesn't make sense for us to sit here in the office all day," Donna Sue said. "Unless you think a new client might come in."

Dwayne grinned. "Like some sexy blond babe who's in trouble, you mean? Like maybe she's got a gat in her purse and a blackmailer on her tail?"

Donna Sue reached for her purse—which didn't have a gat in it—and said, "On the other hand, maybe we *should* go back home for the day."

"Fine with me. I've already got the sexiest blond babe in Wichita right here."

That got him a smile and out of any trouble he might have been in for joshing with her.

The couple went down on the elevator and recrossed the street to the parking garage. They got into the Nash station wagon and drove out to head for their apartment.

"I'm looking forward to dancing!" Donna Sue said happily.

"Oh god!" Dwayne moaned. Dancing had never been his strong suit.

"Dwayne Wheeler, you *will* dance with me and I'm not kidding!"

He knew it wouldn't do any good to argue with that.

IT WAS EARLY EVENING WHEN DWAYNE AND Donna Sue arrived at the Roadhouse Nightclub on the outskirts of Wichita. Dwayne had called in reservations and they were welcomed at the door by the greeters and bouncers Jack Wallace and Dennis Tarball. The Wheelers' name was written on the night's guest lists, and Jack and Dennis had been waiting for them.

"It's been a while since you've been here, guys," Jack said.

"We're glad to see you," Dennis said with a happy grin. "Elmer told us to tell you to go to his office when you showed up."

"Ah hah!" Dwayne said. "That means this is going to be a grand evening!" He took Donna Sue's arm. "Let's go, honey!"

The couple went through the entrance and past the bar to Elmer Pettibone's office. Dwayne knocked on the door. There was a vocal invitation for their entrance and they went inside.

Elmer Pettibone was seated behind his desk. He got up and walked around to shake hands with Dwayne and kiss Donna on the cheek. "I was happy when the maître d' showed me the guest list for tonight. I want to talk to you two this evening about a certain subject that will interest you." He picked up the phone and punched a button. "My guests are here."

He hung up and walked to the door and opened it. "Come along."

Elmer had a special table he used for his favorite guests. It was in a dining room with a one-way window looking out over the rest of the club. When they walked in, he winked at Donna Sue. "Don't worry, kiddo. I've got another table out there where you can sit between dances after we finish eating here."

"Thank God!" Donna Sue said with a smile. "I was afraid I wouldn't get to dance with this husband of mine tonight."

They sat down around the table and two waiters came in with fruit salads. After that was consumed by the diners, the Roadhouse Nightclub's specialty of fricasseed beef and fried potatoes were served. The wine was an expensive pinot noir that was highly acclaimed as the finest of the coastal vineyards of California.

After the waiters withdrew, Elmer poured the wine, then sat back and took a few sips and then some bites of the beef. After chewing and swallowing, he said, "Okay, let me tell you about my taxi fleet. I've just about got what I want. I'm calling it the *Speed-O Taxi Service*." He took a few more bites and then looked over at Dwayne. "By the way, your buddy Jerry Owens is my second-in-command."

"That's great, Elmer!"

"And now here is what's gonna be the best thing. I'm putting in a radio communications system. The two other city cabs—*Wichita Taxi Service* and the *Chisolm Cabs*—have to rely on the telephone."

"Mmm," Dwayne mused. "That's kind of an old fashion cumbersome method, isn't it? The best thing they got is when the bellboys in the Riverview Hotel call for liquor and prostitutes that their guests want."

"Exactly!" Elmer said. "There's no way for a taxi company to go contact their vehicles for rides. They have to be hailed. And I've already pulled a couple of drivers from the local cab companies. Pretty soon, *Speed-O Taxi Service* will be the only taxis on Wichita's streets."

Dwayne took a swig of wine. "You'll be making enemies, Elmer."

"That'll fade away quick enough. The drivers won't want to work for anybody but me."

"Harry and Dennis Walton are still your mechanics, right?" Dwayne asked.

"You bet. Them brothers are old, but nobody else can match their skill when it comes to automotive nuts and bolts."

The supper turned to reminiscing about past days for an hour, then Dwayne and Donna Sue said good night to Elmer and went down to the dance floor.

———

Dwayne and Donna Sue left the club at about two a.m. They were riding down Edgemore Street when Donna Sue said, "Elmer's a pretty selfish guy, isn't he?"

"I don't think so," Dwayne said as he glanced over at her in surprise, not taking his eyes off the road for long. "He's a pretty good guy as far as I'm concerned."

"That's because you've always been agreeing with him and his ideas."

"Well, why wouldn't I? I made a lot of money running whiskey for Elmer Pettibone, and I appreciate it. He's a sharp guy, always ahead of the game."

"You told him yourself he was asking for trouble by trying to take over the taxi business in Wichita, Dwayne. Why do you think he was talking about it tonight? He's expecting problems, too, whether he'll admit it or not, and when they come up, he'll expect you to do something about them."

Dwayne didn't have any answer for that. He knew Donna Sue might be right. The couple fell into an uneasy silence as they drove through the night.

CHAPTER 2

For the next week, Dwayne was working on a caper that involved an employee who was cheating on his employer at the cash register. It was a shoe store situated in a shopping center. Dwayne spied on the guy and turned over the findings after a week of observation.

The next day was an empty one for Dwayne and Donna Sue. Donna Sue was going over her books when she heard some scuffling outside in the hall. She got up and went out to see what was going on.

Two women were watching a janitor hanging a sign on the door directly across from the detective's office. It read:

HOLLYWOOD ACTING AND MODELING STUDIO

They looked over at Donna Sue, and both smiled. "Hello, there," the brunette said.

"Hello," Donna Sue replied. "What's this?"

"We're opening a school of acting and modeling like

the sign says. My name is Gwendolyn Haversham." She spoke in an English accent as she turned and indicated her friend. "And this is my cute little partner, Claudine Gennette. She is French and very musically talented."

"I see," Donna Sue said.

"We have contracts with various moving picture studios," said Claudine, who was a petite redhead. "We are moving into this office because of its large size. The walls are padded, so our interior will be quiet. I play the piano."

"That is very interesting!" Donna Sue said. She nodded toward the door of the office behind her. "We're a detective agency."

The two women looked at each other. "A detective agency?" Gwendolyn asked. "Is that a police station where you work?"

"Oh, no," Donna Sue said. "My husband is a *private* detective. I'm his secretary."

Having heard voices in the hallway, Dwayne sauntered out of the office and joined the group. "What's up?" he asked as he slipped his hands in his trouser pockets.

"We hope to get a few movie stars and models in Wichita," Claudine said.

"I'm impressed!" Dwayne remarked. "Sounds good to me."

"Well, you'll have to excuse us," Gwendolyn said. "We have to fix up our studio and then put advertisements in the newspapers."

Dwayne said, "If you want to get on the radio, I know a guy on the KFH station here in Wichita. He interviews people that are very interesting in our fair city."

Gwendolyn's eyes opened wide. "Can you get him to interview us?"

"He's open for anybody as long as they've got a good

story to tell," Dwayne said. "His name is Harold Hopper. Give him a call and mention my name."

"What *is* your name?" Gwendolyn asked.

Donna Sue was getting leery about her husband being so nice to the two attractive women. He just couldn't help but try to charm good-looking females. He had tried to tell her that would be part of the private detective handbook...if there was a private detective handbook.

"His name is Dwayne Wheeler." She turned to him. "Give her your business card."

"Thank you," Gwendolyn said. "Let's see, I shall remember it is Harold Hopper at KFH. As soon as we get a phone this afternoon, I shall give him a call."

Donna Sue took Dwayne's arm. "We wish you luck." She looked at her hubby. "Come on, Dwayne. There's work to do."

"So long, ladies," Dwayne said over his shoulder.

They were about to return to their office when the freight elevator opened with two movers pushing a piano toward the newcomers' office.

———

ELMER PETTIBONE PUT ANNOUNCEMENTS IN THE *Wichita Eagle* and *Wichita Beacon* newspapers about the *Speed-O Taxi Service*. He played up the radio communication that would be linked to those in the taxis. The owners of the *Wichita Taxi Service* and *Chisolm Cabs* were worried. The people calling in to *Speed-O* could get cabs coming directly to their homes. And already several of their drivers had gone over to *Speed-O*.

Trouble was brewing, all right.

———

AFTER DWAYNE TOLD THEM ABOUT THE RADIO advertising, Gwendolyn Haversham and Claudine Gennette decided to get in touch with Harold Hopper at Radio Station KFH the next day.

When Hopper was contacted by the *Hollywood Acting and Modeling Studio,* he was flabbergasted. This was a contract with the big shots as far as he was concerned. Hopper changed his schedule around to get the two women on the air.

Gwendolyn and Claudine showed up at seven o'clock for the eight o'clock broadcast and found that Hopper had arranged to have a sumptuous bite to eat in his outer office. Several platters of appetizers had been set out on a table covered with a snowy white linen cloth.

"I had this nosh to nibble on while we discussed what the broadcast would be like," he told the visitors as he waved a hand at the table.

The food was actually the best that the kitchen of the *Prairie Wind Golf and Tennis Club* offered, and Hopper made it sound as if it were something he did quite a lot. Actually, the radio station wouldn't put up the money, so Hopper had to pay for it all himself. That didn't bother him, however, since he viewed this as a chance to get into either Hollywood or Los Angeles radio.

After he and the two women had put some delicious delicacies on their plates, he poured the excellent champagne he had gotten from a bootlegger. They all sat down.

"Now tell me about your operation," Hopper said.

Gwendolyn took a swallow of the champagne then answered him. "What we are," she said, "is an outlet of many studios. You know, Metro-Goldwyn-Mayer, Warner Brothers, RKO Productions and others, of course."

"Of course," Hopper agreed.

"You see, our business is finding talented young

women out in America who would be perfect for the movies. The Hollywood bigwigs want to get away from the kind of girls who swarm around the studios like moths to a flame. Do you get my drift?"

"Of course," Hopper said. "What sort of fashion and acting will be taught to the Wichita hopefuls?"

Gwendolyn glanced over to Claudine Gennette. "You tell him, Claudine."

"Certainly, Gwendolyn. At first we practice modeling to teach the right ways to walk and dress. During other lessons, we teach them makeup. The next step is the singing and dancing."

Hopper was getting very, very interested. "Do they all sing or just those with the acting talent?"

"Oh, they *all* must display their musical endowments," Claudine said. "And I play the piano for them."

"I bet you're good at that," Hopper said.

"She is wonderful at it," Gwendolen stated.

"After all that, we see what their real talents are," Claudine said. "We have twenty movie scripts for them to read. That is where Gwendolyn shines."

"Yes. We have five of each script, making a hundred of all kinds so that the real talented can show their natural ability."

"That's so interesting!" Hopper said. "How long are your courses?"

"A year mostly," Gwendolyn replied. "It depends on how fast our students learn."

"I see," Hopper said. "Well, I am amazed." He looked at his watch. "We've got a half hour before the broadcast... and I think it's going to be great!"

———

THE NEXT DAY AFTER HOPPER'S PROGRAM, A LOT of Wichita mothers rushed to the WKH Building to enroll their darling daughters in the *Hollywood Acting and Modeling Studio*.

Donna Sue went to the door and looked out at the line of mothers and daughters. She turned around and walked over to Dwayne. "Let me tell you something. There's gonna be a lot of disappointed females before this is over."

CHAPTER 3

Oskar and Borghild Hanson and their ten-year-old daughter Kari were Norwegians living in Norway during the German occupation. Oskar was an aircraft guidance instrument expert being forced to work for the Nazis. Consequently, the Norwegian underground managed to kill a few Germans in a raid designed to rescue the Hansons. They pulled it off and smuggled the family over to the United States. Upon arrival, the US Air Force assigned Oskar to use his skills working in the Boeing Aircraft Factory in Wichita, Kansas.

After the war ended, Oskar and Borghild became naturalized American citizens, and he continued working at Boeing. Their daughter Kari, now eighteen, automatically became an American when her parents became citizens. The Norwegian American family lived happily in Wichita and even enjoyed two weeks over the Christmas season going to Lutsen Mountain, Minnesota, to ski, which had been one of their favorite activities back in Norway.

Kari's best friend was a girl her age named Jennie

Watson. They lived across the street from each other, but unfortunately, their houses were on Murdock Avenue. That street was the dividing line between Wichita's high school attendance zones. Kari attended Wichita High School East on the south side of Murdock, and Jennie attended Wichita High School North on the other side of the street.

Both girls were straight-A students and were beautiful young ladies. All the boys worshipped them, but they were not interested in any of their potential suitors. To those serious girls, romance and dating seemed idiotic.

Kari and Jennie were also very athletic young women and were captains of their girls' field hockey teams. Every year the Wichita High School East Blue Aces and the Wichita High School North Redskins—the only two public high schools in the city—played for a championship in the Wichita University football stadium.

The 1948 game was scheduled to take place just before the first semester came to a close. It was on an evening when the football field was available. The field for the contest was one hundred yards long, and that was the same as field hockey. The lines marking the football games could not be removed. However, it was alright for the goals to be set up at the end of each field. These were two upright posts with crossbars. A net was strung up on the rear of that.

The games were played by teams of eleven, consisting of ten field players and one goalkeeper. Hockey sticks were used to hit the balls into the goals or to teammates running down the field. There were two periods of thirty-five minutes and a fifteen-minute halftime interval.

So far, the teams were tied and eager to get a win. Kari and Jennie were fond of each other, but when they were on the field, they played hard to score their schools' victories.

The stadium filled with students and families attending the contest. There were automobiles parked outside the stadium with blue and red banners on them. Parents hurrying into the stadium carried pennants with the color of their daughters' teams. Also, both Blue Aces and Redskins had their cheerleaders to add to the excitement.

At six o'clock, the two referees signaled both the high schools' two female coaches to come out to the center of the field to shake hands. The crowd of parents was loud and called out "Go Blue Aces!" or "Go Redskins!" The coaches waved at their boosters and then went back to the sidelines.

Now the two team captains went out into the center of the field to meet the referees. Then the game was ready to begin. Kari and Jennie put the ends of their hockey sticks down on the grass to touch close together. The tension was crackling in the air, then the referee blew his whistle and the game was on.

Kari got the ball on her stick and knocked it over to one of the Blue Ace forwards, who passed it over to a midfielder. She took it down the field as both teams raced over the turf.

After a few vicious but slickly executed passes, Jennie Watson scored. The Redskin side of the field shouted in glee. The Blue Ace goalkeeper took the ball and knocked it out to her teammates. After that, the players on both sides stole the ball several times and the game action surged back and forth for long minutes before Kari put the ball in the goal and the game was tied. Play continued, the goalkeepers each made several good saves, and time ticked away on the scoreboard until the end of the half with no more scoring.

During the fifteen-minute halftime interval, freshman boys carried water out to the players. The girl athletes got a kick out of that. Then it was time for the second period. Once again, Kari and Jennie placed their hockey sticks next to each other and stared into each other's eyes.

The referee blew his whistle, and once again, the battle was on.

The game was rough and tough and as the players grew tired, more and more balls went into the goal. The lead changed hands several times, but neither team was able to dominate. Finally, the game ended with a tie of 12-12. Kari and Jennie, sweating and breathing hard, hugged each other, then turned to shake the hands of the opposing team. The fathers of the players on both teams were upset by the tie, but the mothers were proud of their girls.

———

ELMER PETTIBONE DUG INTO A LARGE PART OF his hidden bootleg stash to help finance his growing taxi service. The first thing he did was to have his taxi cabs painted bright red, so that no one could miss seeing them as they cruised the streets of Wichita. The name *Speed-O Taxi Service* was lettered in yellow on the doors. All had radio communications installed in the vehicles.

His next task was to get his shortwave radio set up on the top of the Ellis Singleton Building at 221 South Broadway. A want-ad in the newspapers had gotten him three operators: one was an Army veteran with experience in the signal corps, another a navy veteran who had been a third-class radioman on a battleship and a Marine who had been a radio operator in the South Pacific. These men worked seven days and eight-hour shifts a day. Because there were no days off, Elmer paid them seventy dollars a week.

Jerry Owens, now his top aide, had been able to hire a good number of drivers. He did such an effective job that John Stacker's *Wichita Tax Service* and Harold Fox's *Chisolm Cabs* lost all their drivers.

When the time was right, Elmer Pettibone advertised his business in Wichita's two newspapers.

ATTENTION!
THE SPEED-O TAXI SERVICE
IS NOW READY TO SERVE YOU!
WHEN YOU WANT OUR RADIO SERVICE
CALL ATwater 8-0542
A CAB WILL BE AT YOUR FRONT DOOR IN A
FLASH!

Elmer and Jerry waited for the business to boom!

CHAPTER 4

Gwendolyn Haversham and Claudine Ginnette got out of a cab in front of the Riverview Hotel. They walked over to the revolving door and crossed the lobby to the elevator. The operator took them up to the expensive, luxuriously furnished second floor. Gwendolyn went to her room while Claudine walked to the one where she was staying with her lover Jacques Leroux.

Leroux was a tall, husky Frenchman who was exceedingly handsome, making Claudine very jealous of him. He was seated on a reclining chair reading a book and got up to walk over and give her a hug and kiss.

"How did it go today?" he wanted to know.

"Not very well, I am afraid."

Leroux was the pilot for the two women and had flown them into Wichita in a Beechcraft 18 aircraft for the *Hollywood Acting and Modeling Studio*. The Frenchman was not only a pilot but also was an important supervisor in their organization.

"Do not tell me there are no attractive young women in this city," he stated.

"Only brunettes showed up," Claudine said. "But you know what we are looking for, correct?"

"Yes. Blondes and redheads. We cannot waste a lot of time here. I can only hope you and Gwendolyn do well."

"We are doing our best, believe me," Claudine said.

Her lover embraced her. "I am certain that you are."

"I'll go see if Gwendolyn wants to join us for supper in the restaurant downstairs."

———

DONNA SUE WAS AT HER DESK IN THE WKH Building when a young boy walked through the door. She looked at him, figuring he was about twelve years old.

She was polite even though she didn't take him for a potential client. "What can I do for you?"

"I want to see the detective," he said. "I need to hire him."

"What in the world for?"

"There's a guy that bullies me all the time," the kid said. He reached into his pocket and pulled out a dollar bill. "I got money, see?"

Donna Sue grinned. "Yes, I do." She decided she wanted to find out more about the kid. "What school do you go to?"

"Roosevelt Junior High. I'm a seventh grader."

"And who is this bully?"

"He's in the ninth grade and is a big guy."

Donna Sue decided she wanted Dwayne to see this. "Dwayne," she called. "Will you come out here?"

Dwayne laid down the newspaper he was reading and walked out to her desk. "What's going on?"

"This boy," Donna Sue said. "Has a caper for you. And he has a dollar to pay."

Dwayne looked at the kid. "Is that right? So what's your problem?"

"I got a guy that bullies me," he said.

"What's your name?"

"Tommy Carson," he answered. "I'm in the seventh grade at Roosevelt Junior High School. The guy that bullies me is in the ninth grade, and he's big, and his name is Troy Bulski."

"Mmm," Dwayne mused as he hooked his thumbs in the pockets of his vest and looked serious. "And how does he bully you?"

"He hits me, and he grabs me around the neck and rubs my head real hard, and he shakes me and—"

"—wait up, pardner," Dwayne said. He was thoughtful for a moment. "Shouldn't you be in school right now?"

"Yes, but I didn't go today because I wanted to come over here, and I want you to go over to the school and beat Troy up and tell him to stop bullying me."

Dwayne had gone to Roosevelt Junior High himself and didn't like bullies. He wasn't one, but he was one of the toughest guys in the school and had stopped many a bully who was making a weaker boy miserable. At first when he had come out into Donna Sue's office, he had figured this was some kind of joke. He could tell, though, that she was taking it seriously and so he did, too.

"I tell you what, Tommy. I'll take you to school right now, and I'll see what I can do for you."

Tommy held out the dollar bill.

"You don't have to pay me," Dwayne said. He looked over at Donna Sue. "I'm going to look into Tommy's problem."

Donna Sue smiled. "I'm glad you're going to do that, Dwayne. This is an important caper."

He saw the affection and warmth in her eyes and was glad he'd decided to play along.

Dwayne got his hat off the rack and patted Tommy's shoulder. "Come on. My station wagon is across the street in the parking garage."

The drive from downtown to Roosevelt Junior High took ten minutes. He pulled up behind the school building.

"C'mon, Tommy. I know the way to the office," he said as they got out of the car. He chuckled. "I was called in there a lot when I was a student here."

"Really?"

"That's right. I wasn't always Wichita's top private detective and the fine, upstanding citizen you see before you today."

They went up to the second floor and into the office foyer. A female secretary was behind the counter and looked up at them. "May I help you?"

"This is Tommy Carson I have with me," Dwayne said. He put his hand on the boy's shoulder.

"Yes, I'm aware of that. He was listed as absent this morning."

"I would like to talk to the principal, please."

The principal was called, and he came out of his office. "What can I do for you?"

"It's about a small boy who is being bullied by a much bigger boy in this school."

"And who are you?" the principal asked.

Dwayne pulled out his private detective badge. "I'm Dwayne Wheeler."

He said the name as if the principal ought to recognize it, and the way the man's eyes widened told Dwayne that he did.

"Oh! I've heard a lot about you, Mr. Wheeler." He

held out his hand. "I'm John Franklin. Glad to know you. So tell me about this situation."

Dwayne told him about Tommy's problem. Principal Franklin turned to the secretary. "Go fetch Troy Bulski, Miss Applebee."

"Yes, Mr. Franklin."

She went over to the file cabinet and found what room the boy was in at that time. She left the office and in five minutes, came back with Troy Bulski, who was a big, sullen-faced youngster.

"You listen to what Mr. Wheeler here has to say, Troy," Principal Franklin said.

Troy glared and scuffed his feet on the tile floor without saying anything.

"I want to talk to you about your bullying of Tommy Carson here," Dwayne snapped.

"I don't mean nothing," Troy shot back. "It's just having fun."

"Well, it's not having fun for Tommy!"

Troy repeated, "I don't mean nothing."

Principal Franklin stepped into the conversation. "I want you to apologize to Tommy."

Troy mumbled, "I'm sorry." His jaw was tight.

"Ask him to forgive you," Dwayne said.

"Forgive me."

"Well, alright," Tommy said.

With that done, both boys left the office and went to their scheduled rooms.

Dwayne turned to Principal Franklin. "Do you have information on Troy's parents?"

"Certainly." He went to the file cabinet and came back with a card.

Dwayne got the information on Troy Bulski's dad. He worked at the Newly Machine Shop out on George Washington Boulevard south of Pawnee Street. Dwayne handed the card back to the principal.

"I'll go call on his dad."

"Good idea," the principal said. "I'm not sure how sincere Troy's apology was."

"Oh, it wasn't," Dwayne said. "I think I can pretty much promise you that."

He started to turn away, but Franklin stopped him by asking, "Um, Mr. Wheeler...why is a well-known detective such as you involving himself in a minor case of bullying?"

"Tommy's my client," Dwayne said, even though no money had changed hands. "And where my clients are concerned, there are no minor capers."

Dwayne left the school office and went down to his station wagon. It took him twenty minutes to get out to the machine shop where Troy's father worked. He pulled up in front of the building and got out to go inside the shop. The place was roaring with machinery. He looked around, and a man walked over to him.

"What can I do for you?" the man asked, raising his voice to be heard over the noise.

"I'm looking for William Bulski," Dwayne yelled.

"Who should I say is looking for him?"

Dwayne pulled out his badge and held it cupped in the palm of his hand.

"Jesus!" the man said. "Wait here, Officer."

He scurried back into the depths of the shop. A few moments later, a man with a muscular body that had a layer of fat over it approached Dwayne. "Whatcha want?"

"William Bulski?"

"That's right."

"Let's go outside," Dwayne said.

They walked out to the silent outdoors. Bulski was

confused. "What does a cop want with me?"

"I'm not a cop."

"My boss said—"

"I'm a private detective," Dwayne interrupted him. "I never claimed to be a cop. But I can't help what people assume when I show them my badge." Dwayne got down to business. "I talked with Troy about his bullying of a smaller boy."

"Yeah? Which kid?"

"Tommy Carson. I thought you might talk to Troy about it, too."

"Talk about it? I'll talk to that kid of mine with whipping a belt on his ass."

"Wait a minute," Dwayne said. "He apologized to the other kid and said he wouldn't do it anymore. There's no sense in punishing him."

Bulski snarled, "I'll deal with my boy my way!" An angry frown drew his bushy eyebrows down. "What kind of detective are you? I never heard of a private dick who'd get mixed up in school kids picking on each other!"

"Somebody comes to me for help. I try to do what I can for them."

"Yeah, well, butt out of my business."

Dwayne watched him turn around and go back into the shop.

The shamus went over to his station wagon and sat there for a few minutes. He was worried about Troy now. He had figured Troy's dad needed to know what was going on, but he hadn't expected the guy to react in such a surly fashion.

On the other hand, Troy had learned to be a bully somewhere. What better place than home?

Dwayne started the motor and headed for downtown and his office.

CHAPTER 5

Mrs. Borghild Hanson and Mrs. Mary Watson had become worried about the lack of femininity in their daughters' activities. The girls' favorite fun was when they went to the public park at the corner of the street. They loved to run around and through it, and they also pulled themselves up and down on exercise bars.

Mr. Oskar Hanson and Mr. Stanley Watson were not troubled a bit about their girls' liveliness. The fact that Kari and Jennie showed exceptional skill playing field hockey made the men very proud of their daughters.

When advertisements for the *Hollywood Acting and Modeling Studio* were printed in the *Wichita Eagle* and *Wichita Beacon*, they caught the mothers' attention. They got together in the Watson house and decided to take their two daughters over to the WKH Building and enroll them in the courses, thinking it would be good for them. Kari and Jennie were not pleased at all.

"Gee whiz, Mom," Kari whined. "That's just boring stuff!"

"Yeah!" Jennie complained. "Kari and I want to do things outside, not indoors!"

Mrs. Hanson spoke. "Go and put on your prettiest dress, Kari!"

"Jennie! Get upstairs to your bedroom and put that dress on I bought for you!" Mrs. Watson ordered.

———

MRS. WATSON DROVE HER CAR DOWNTOWN WITH Mrs. Hanson and the two girls. She parked a block from the WKH Building and they all got out. The mothers made a last inspection of their daughters, who looked beautiful despite their reluctance to dress up, then walked up the street to the building.

The elevator let them out on the second floor, and they suddenly stopped. The line of other hopeful mothers and daughters was a long one.

Jennie grinned, sensing a way to get out of this. "Let's go home, Mom. We'd have to stand up here for hours."

"Yeah!" Kari happily exclaimed. "You hate standing in line, Ma."

The glare from each mother told them silently that they were not going anywhere.

Inside the *Hollywood Acting and Modeling Studio*, Gwendolyn Haversham and Claudine Ginnette were ready to scream. The latest candidates—a fat mother and daughter—had been turned down.

"I'm beginning to think that Wichita, Kansas, hasn't another single pretty girl except the two we already have," Gwendolyn said. "Oh! How I wish for more blondes and redheads."

"That's all we can choose for what we must have,"

Claudine uttered as she lit a cigarette. "Let us wait for at least fifteen minutes, or I shall go insane!"

They fell into somber moods of depression. Claudine finally tapped her cigarette out in the ashtray. She stood up. "Here I go again."

The little French woman stepped out into the corridor. She started to invite the next two candidates in line to enter the office, but her eyes spotted two girls—one blond and one redhead—at the end of the queue. She immediately walked down toward them. The closer she got, the happier she was.

"Hello!" Claudine greeted them. "Will you please accompany me?" She ignored the resentful looks she got from some of the other mothers and daughters waiting in the hallway.

Mrs. Hanson and Mrs. Watson were excited that their daughters had been singled out. *Miss* Hanson and *Miss* Watson were not. But short of making a break for it and angering their mothers, there was nothing they could do. Claudine led them past the other hopefuls. She stood at the door and ushered the four in.

Gwendolyn Haversham almost fell out of her chair. She literally jumped up. "I say! Hello! I am most pleased to meet you!"

The mothers were happily surprised, but the daughters were still resentful about the situation.

Gwendolyn asked the girls to walk across the room. "Look at you!" she exclaimed as they did. "You are beautiful!"

Claudine giggled happily. "You are just what we want and need."

Gwendolyn walked over to a desk and pulled out cards that gave permission for their mothers to let them study at the *Hollywood Acting and Modeling Studio*.

She stepped out into the hall and told the other mothers and daughters the *Hollywood Acting and Modeling Studio* was no longer accepting new students.

———

THE WINNERS OF THE WICHITA TRYOUTS WERE Kari Hanson and Jennie Watson, as well as Molly McNally, a redhead, who was a senior at Saint James Catholic School; Caroline Taylor, a redhead, who was a senior at East High and Rachel Carlson, a blond, who was also a senior at North High. Lined up as they were in the office, the five of them were stunningly beautiful.

Gwendolyn looked at the five mothers, who stood to one side with proud, pleased expressions on their faces. "We have some rules we must tell you about," Gwendolyn began in a stern voice. "Number one is that the girls must not have boyfriends."

"I have one," Molly McNally said. "But I'm sort of tired of him."

"Will you break up with the boy?"

"Of course!" Molly agreed without a second's hesitation.

"Excellent! The next rule is a sensitive one. I must mention that the girls must be virgins." Gwendolyn looked carefully at the mothers.

They all nodded their heads that their daughters were pure.

"We would also like the girls to bring sack lunches. That way, we won't waste time in our lessons."

The mothers agreed.

"Also," Gwendolyn said. "I'm afraid that your mothers cannot come to visit our training."

Again the mothers agreed.

"Wonderful," Gwendolyn said. She smiled as she looked at the girls. "We will see you next Saturday and many more."

———

IT WAS FIVE A.M. WHEN THE ELDERLY BROTHERS, Harry and Dennis Walton, showed up at the *Speed-O* Taxi Service garage to begin checking out the vehicles for the day's business.

The brothers stepped up to the door and found it open. "What's this all about?" Dennis asked. They went inside and noticed the taxis were all leaning slightly to their right side.

"Will you look at that?" Harry said.

"Yeah," Dennis said.

They walked up to the vehicles and found the trouble. "Hey!" Harry said. "All them taxis' tires on the right sides has been punctured."

"I'm gonna go call Elmer," Dennis said. He walked over to the office and picked up the telephone on the desk to dial Elmer Pettibone's house number. After six rings, the call was answered.

"Mmm, hullo," said a sleepy voice.

"Izzat you, Elmer?"

"Huh?"

Dennis repeated, "Izzat you, Elmer?"

"Oh, yeah," Elmer said. "What's up, Dennis?"

"Ever' right side tire on the taxis has been punctured."

Elmer was shocked. "What the hell! I'll be right down, Dennis."

Fifteen minutes had passed when Elmer drove up in his brand new Cadillac and honked at the garage door.

Elmer opened the large entrance and Elmer gunned his car in. He braked to a stop, turned the ignition key and got out. He rushed over to the taxis.

"Son of a bitch! Son of a fucking bitch." He turned a furious, wide-eyed glare on the brothers. "Who the hell done this?"

"We don't know," Harry said.

"Goddammit, Harry!" Elmer spit out. "I know you don't know who did it."

"What're we gonna do?"

Elmer thought a moment. "Okay! Get the good tires off half of them taxis and swap them out with the flats on the other taxis. At least we can get half of the bunch out on the streets working. Then I want you two to order more tires."

The brothers began to follow the instructions as Elmer went over to the office. "I'm gonna call Dwayne Wheeler!" He stopped. "Wait a minute! He ain't gonna be in his office. It's too early." He took a deep breath and then remembered something. "Oh! I got his apartment number in my Rolodex."

He went to his desk, looked up Dwayne's number, and dialed it.

The phone rang several times before Donna Sue's sleepy voice answered. "Hello."

"Hi, Donna Sue. This is me, Elmer. Wake up, Dwayne, and tell him that some of my taxis have been sabotaged."

"He's awake now. Here he is."

Dwayne's voice came over the phone. "What's up, Elmer?"

"All of my taxis' tires on the right side have been sabotaged," Elmer said. "They're flat as can be. Somebody must've took a knife or an icepick to them. I want you to come over to the garage right away."

"Okay," Dwayne said. "I'll be there as quick as I can. I've got some other things to do first."

"Okay, I'll wait," Elmer said with a sigh. "The damage has already been done anyhow."

CHAPTER 6

Dwayne got over to the *Speed-O Taxi Service* at noon. He parked outside the door and walked to the garage. He made a quick study of the broken lock, then went inside.

Harry and Dennis were busy changing the rest of the tires on the cabs and both waved hellos to him. Elmer Pettibone saw Dwayne from his office and hurried out.

"Where the hell have you been?" Elmer demanded.

"Me and Donna Sue had some important legal papers to finish up and mail off," Dwayne said.

"Okay, I guess," Elmer replied. "C'mon, and I'll show you the busted lock on the door. That's how the crooks got in."

"I already looked at it," Dwayne said. "And it wasn't busted *in*, it was busted *out*. It seems to me the work was done by somebody who was inside last night."

"Okay," Elmer said. "But that doesn't make any sense. It was these cabs that were getting their regular scheduled maintenance. I rotate 'em that way. Six cabs at a time. The rest are out picking up rides."

"I tell you what, Elmer. If these were brought in, then one or more of the cabbies in that group stayed behind and hid. Then, when the garage was empty, the guy slashed the tires and broke out the door to escape."

Elmer's eyes widened. "By God, Dwayne! You're right!"

"So here's what we're gonna do. You check the names of the drivers who turned in those particular cabs. When it's their turn to come in again and **there are** more punctured tires, then somebody in that group will have done the foul deed."

"Keep talking, Dwayne."

"If I hide in here when those guys are slashing tires, I can jump out and yell boo at them."

"Way to go, Dwayne! It'll be three weeks before this particular group rotates back."

"I tell you what, Elmer. I'd like to have Jerry Owens with me on this caper. Him and me were partner drivers in those yellow cigarette trucks. I got a lot of respect for him."

"By God, Dwayne! I'll do just that. You betcha!"

————

ON THE FIRST SATURDAY MORNING OF CLASSES, Gwendolyn Haversham and Claudine Ginnette decided to let the parents and daughters show up for a *Hollywood Acting and Modeling Studio* orientation. Gwendolyn invited them in and the guests were surprised to see a handsome man seated with Claudine Ginnette.

The invitees settled down, and Gwendolyn went to the rostrum. "Good morning, ladies, gentlemen, and daughters. We are pleased to have this opportunity to make our acquaintance with you all. At this time, I would like to introduce Jacques Leroux, who is one of the executives of *Hollywood Acting and Modeling*. By the way, Mr. Leroux served in the French underground during the war. He fought the Nazis and was awarded the Legion of Honor for bravery."

There was applause from the fathers who were all veterans of World War II.

"And," Gwendolyn added. "He is flying the Metro-Goldwyn-Mayer studio airplane. He flew Claudine and me here from Hollywood to Wichita. When they finish your courses, he will fly us and the girls to California. That will be when they get their screen tests. And I just wager they will pass them and be ready to star in movies."

Mrs. Watson raised her hand. "When will that happen?"

"It depends on the result of their studies," Gwendolyn replied.

"Can we go with them?" another mother asked.

"No, I am afraid not. Now Jacques Leroux has a welcome for you."

Leroux stepped up behind the podium. "Hello, everyone. I am most happy to be here in your beautiful city. You have convinced us that we can now spread out into this great nation to seek more gifted young ladies who can become movie stars. I see the bright young ladies of Wichita, Kansas, here, and I am so happy to be able to fly them to their glory of movie roles and the money they can earn. Thank you."

The guests applauded. Then a door opened and a cart of delicacies was wheeled in by a waiter from one of Wichita's best Continental Grills.

Everyone got up to go over to put nosh-type food on paper plates. Jacques Leroux was bombarded with questions from the fathers about what kind of movies their daughters would be in and how much money they would earn.

"The actresses will be paid six figures for their work," Leroux replied, but he evaded the questions about what sort of movies the girls would perform in.

The mothers were worried more about their daughters' safety. They wanted to know the type of clothing they would be wearing in the movies. One wanted to know what sort of men they would meet in Hollywood society.

"You hear all sorts of things about the men out there being such...such wolves!"

"I assure you, madam, actresses are looked after and guarded by the studios," Leroux assured them. "After all, they have an investment in those girls. I give you my word. They will be as safe as if they were in church!"

———

DWAYNE, JERRY OWENS, AND ELMER PETTIBONE were hidden in the darkness of Elmer's office. Harry and Dennis Walton were out in the garage waiting for the six cabbies who would drop off their vehicles for maintenance to be done the next morning.

A few minutes passed, then the outer doors opened, and the cabs were driven in. Dwayne got to his feet and eased over to a spot where he could see the activity. The drivers got out and headed for the doors.

The shamus silently counted, "One...two...three... four..." to himself.

Harry and Dennis got the cabs lined up for the work they would be doing the next morning. With that taken care of, they went over to the door and the two mechanics locked the portals, then left the garage.

Dwayne drew his .45 auto pistol and nodded to Jerry and Elmer. "There's two still out there somewhere," he said so quietly he couldn't be overheard outside the office. "Let's wait and see what happens."

Darkness came and the lights of a couple of flashlights appeared. Then there were popping sounds and the hiss of air escaping.

Dwayne led the way out of the office, holding his pistol while Elmer and Jerry followed him. All three walked softly, then eased around to the right side of the cabs. They saw two young men about to slash the tires of the third and fourth vehicles.

"Hold it!" Dwayne said, aiming his pistol at them. "Raise your hands!"

They were two young men who were wearing their *Speed-O Taxi Service* uniforms. With a .45 pointed right at them and probably looking like a cannon to their startled eyes, they had no choice but to obey the shamus.

Elmer was flabbergasted. "Why the hell are you puncturing those tires?"

One of them answered, "We're the sons of the owners of the *Wichita Taxi Service* and the *Chisolm Cabs.*"

"Stacker and Fox?" Elmer exclaimed. "This schoolboy harassment won't do you any good. Did your dads put you up to this?"

Bob Stacker answered, "They don't know nothing about it."

"That's right," Jeff Fox replied. "We wanted to get even with you for what you done to our dads' businesses."

"Put your hands behind your backs," Dwayne ordered. He moved in and cuffed them efficiently, saying, "You boys are gonna be behind bars before this night is over."

CHAPTER 7

Dwayne Wheeler and Elmer Pettibone were standing before Judge William Dodge in his courtroom. This case involved the incident of the damage done in the *Speed-O Taxi Service* garage. Bobby Stacker and Jeff Fox had just pleaded guilty on their part.

Their court-appointed attorney, Carl Banter, spoke up. "I haven't had time to discuss this case with my clients, Your Honor. Therefore I'm withdrawing their guilty pleas."

"So be it," the judge said. "What is this charge all about?"

"They're accused of puncturing some tires on cabs, Your Honor," the attorney said. "I haven't had the opportunity to determine the facts of the matter."

"I see. Since they both pled guilty, the facts seem pretty straightforward." The judge cleared his throat. "But you have withdrawn those pleas, as is your right, Mr. Banter. Is the plaintiff present?"

Elmer Pettibone spoke up as he got to his feet. "That'd be me, Your Honor."

"Well, well," Judge Dodge said. "You've been in my court many times, Elmer. **And** this time, you're the accuser rather than the accused."

"That's right, Your Honor."

The judge looked past Elmer. "Well! Here is Detective Dwayne Wheeler. Are you on Elmer's side?"

"Yes, sir," Dwayne said.

The door to the courtroom opened and John Stacker and Harold Fox hurried down the aisle and through the gate in the railing that separated the defense and prosecution tables from the spectator seats. "What's going on here?" Stacker asked when the two men reached the defense table.

"We just heard that our boys were in court," Fox added. "Who's trying to railroad them?"

Judge Dodge banged his gavel. "Order in the court! No one is being railroaded. Not in my courtroom! Who are you gentlemen?"

"I'm John Stacker, former owner of the *Wichita Taxi Service*."

"And I'm Harold Fox, former owner of the *Chisolm Cabs Service*."

"Are you kin to these young people here?"

"Yes, Your Highness," John Stacker said.

"That should be Your *Honor*!" the judge admonished him.

"They're our sons," Fox stated. "And we want to know what they're doing in here."

Carl Banter spoke up. "I'm their attorney. These young men have been charged with puncturing tires on some *Speed-O* cabs. We were about to find out if they actually did it and why."

Bobby Stacker raised his hand. "We done it to get even with *Speed-O* for busting up our dads' businesses."

John Stacker glared at his son. "Who told you to do that?"

"Me and Jeff thought it up all by ourselves."

"We ain't starving, Bobby," Harold Fox said. "Me and your dad have done a lot of buying war bonds and other investments throughout the years."

Elmer Pettibone looked at the judge. "I tell you what, Your Honor. I'll withdraw the charges if them two boys will pay for the damage they did. And I reckon I won't fire them from the *Speed-O* if they want to keep driving for me. They was just mad about what happened to their dads, and I guess I can't blame them too much for that." He turned and looked at Dwayne Wheeler. "They ain't criminals no more, Dwayne."

"Wait a minute, Elmer," Judge Dodge stated. "I'm the person who says who's criminals and who's not."

"Okay, Your Honor," Elmer said. "I didn't mean to overstep. I just don't want no war with these guys." He nodded toward Stacker and Fox.

The judge banged his gavel. "Case dismissed!"

———

THE GIRLS' SATURDAY TRAINING SESSIONS IN THE *Hollywood Acting and Modeling Studio* included sack lunches made by their mothers. The trading of sandwiches was alive with laughter and fun for the five girls.

Claudine Ginnette had plenty of modern song sheets for them to sing. The cute little French pianist played "This Can't Be Love," "Serenade In Blue," "I've Got A Date With A Dream," "Anapola," "Bye Blue Blues," and others.

Gwendolyn Haversham had the girls singing solo,

duet, and trio to get a good practice in their musical studies.

Then there was the reading of movie scripts. One was a **W**estern, and everyone laughed when Jennie Watson tried to speak like a cowboy. Kari Hanson had a script that called for her weeping, and she could only go so far to keep from laughing. Molly McNally, Caroline Taylor, and Rachel Carlson were acting out a threesome of a trio of women in a restaurant. They couldn't keep from giggling when they were supposed to show anger.

Gwendolyn finally grew impatient and scolded the girls. "Listen to me! Do you think your silliness will get you a place in the movies? Do you think some director of a drama would want to put you in his pictures? Do you think you can laugh and stumble around in a serious crime picture?"

The five girls were surprised by her seriousness and quickly realized that Hollywood was not going to be exactly what they had expected.

———

DWAYNE AND DONNA SUE HAD AN UNEXPECTED walk-in client one Saturday morning. Donna Sue looked up at the man from her desk and could see he was distressed. She immediately called for Dwayne.

He came out of his office and quickly sized the visitor up. "What can we do to help you?"

The man was close to weeping in fear. "My sister is in danger."

"From who?" Dwayne inquired.

"Her husband...my brother-in-law."

"Come back with me to my desk," Dwayne invited.

The pair went to the rear of the office and sat down. "What's your name?"

"Leonard Thompson."

"Okay, Leonard. Take a deep breath or two. Then tell me the facts."

"Whew," Thompson said a few times. "My brother-in-law has threatened to kill my sister Dora. This is because she wants a divorce."

"I take it that it isn't a happy marriage," Dwayne said, beginning to take notes.

"He beats her up a lot for any minor thing that pisses him off."

"Has she gotten a legal paper for him to stay away from her?" Dwayne inquired.

"It didn't do any good," Leonard said. "So I went over to their house while he was at work. Me and Dora got a lot of her things and their son and we went back to my place."

"You said *son*. Then he isn't a baby."

"No, he's fourteen years old and scared to death of his dad."

"What's the husband's name?" Dwayne asked.

"William Bulski."

Dwayne looked up sharply from the notes he'd been making. "Where does he work?"

"Newly Machine Shop," Leonard answered. "It's out on—"

"—George Washington Boulevard south of Pawnee," Dwayne said. "I know the place...and the guy. William Bulski. So he's threatening his wife?"

"Yeah."

"I called on him out there about his kid Troy being a bully. He said he was going to give him a whipping."

"Troy is a bully, and he's learned how to do it from his

dad beating him up," Leonard said. "The kid is only trying to get even for his treatment at home by bullying other kids. It's terrible!"

"It sure is," Dwayne said. "Has Dora got someplace to go that he doesn't know about?"

"No. I'm her only relative in Wichita."

"Where is she now?" Dwayne asked.

"My house."

"Well, we've got to change that. That's the first place he'll look for her, and you can't stay there all the time to protect her." Dwayne didn't add that he could tell by looking, Leonard Thompson was no match physically for a brute like Bulski. He got up. "Let's go get Doris. Then we can go to Roosevelt Junior High School and pick up Troy. I suppose that's where he is?"

"Yeah, he still has to go to school, or we'll have the truant officer on our necks."

Dwayne went to Donna Sue's desk. "I got to get a mother and kid to the Salvation Army." He looked over at Leonard. "They have a special place for beaten women."

"Thank God!" he said, sobbing in relief. "I didn't know about that."

Dwayne and Leonard walked over to the parking garage and got into the Nash station wagon. Their first stop would be to get Dora. When they pulled up to their destination after following the directions Leonard gave him, Dwayne saw a frightened woman looking out the front window.

"That's Dora," Leonard said.

The two men went to the door and were let in. Leonard was in a hurry. "Dora, get the stuff you brought with you for you and Troy."

Dora was confused. "What's going on, Leonard?"

"This is Dwayne Wheeler, a private detective. He's

going to take you to a safe place where you'll be hidden from Bill."

It didn't take long to gather the things for Dora and her son. They went out to the Nash and Dwayne headed for the school. When they arrived, Dwayne led the way up the stairs to the office.

They saw Principal Franklin walking down the hall. He stopped when he saw them. "Well! What have we here?"

"We're here to pick up Troy Bulski," Dwayne said. "These folks are his mother and uncle."

"Why do you want to pull Troy out of class?"

"We're on our way to the Salvation Army," Dwayne said. "She has legal papers that her husband is to stay away from her. Bulski won't do it, so she had to leave her house. Troy will have to go with her."

"Wait here," the principal said. "I'll get him for you."

Ten minutes later, he returned with a bewildered Troy. The boy looked at Dwayne. "I ain't bullied nobody!"

"This ain't nothing about that," Leonard said to his nephew. "We're taking you to where your dad can't beat you or your mother anymore."

"Thanks," Dwayne said to Principal Franklin. "I'll keep in touch with you."

"Please do. We'll have to make arrangements so that Troy can attend school safely."

They all got into the Nash, and Dwayne drove to the Salvation Army Building. When they got out, he helped Leonard and Dora with their belongings and they went through the back door. A Salvation Army lady saw them come in. She was Major Mary Johnson, and she knew Dwayne because of his relationship with the late Tommy Brady who had belonged to the Christian organization.

"Hello, Dwayne," she said, looking at Leonard, Dora, and Troy. "What brings you here?"

"This is Dora Bulski and her son Troy," Dwayne said. "Dora has been treated rough by her husband after she asked him for a divorce. Her brother Leonard came to me to get her to a safe place."

"Oh, dear!" Major Mary said. "We can certainly get her to a secure spot where she'll be treated very well." She paused. "Does Dora have a paper that indicates her husband mustn't come close to her?"

"She does," Leonard said.

"That makes a difference in her stay," Major Mary said. "We can treat her and her boy very well."

Dwayne turned to Leonard. "Let's get you back to your car."

Leonard kissed Dora and Troy, then went out the back door with Dwayne. The shamus drove to where Leonard had parked his car. Then he headed for the WKH Building. When he walked into his office, Donna Sue was curious.

"How did it go, Dwayne?"

Dwayne explained what he had been doing during his absence. Then he lit a Lucky Strike. "I'm gonna go after that son of a bitch, Bill Bulski, and drag his rotten ass to jail."

"I don't blame you, sweetheart."

CHAPTER 8

E lmer Pettibone had finally reached the finishing touches on his *Speed-O Taxi Service*. He enlarged his radio station, hired two more women to take calls over the phones, and ordered a half dozen more cabs.

Elmer and Jerry Owens refurnished the office in the garage. Those two men were veteran bootleggers, along with Dwayne Wheeler. Their last unlawful operation had been hauling illegal cigarettes that had no US government stamps. The two elderly brothers, Harry and Dennis Walton, were also involved in those illegal activities.

Since the conclusion of that scheme, Dwayne had concentrated on legitimate private detective business, for the most part. If some shady opportunity came along that offered the potential of a good payday, he would have to consider it, but he had worked hard to establish his reputation as a detective, so he preferred sticking to those jobs.

As for the members of the Wichita public, some of them were aware of Elmer's questionable background, but were delighted with the new cab rides despite that. They could get a cab within fifteen minutes and still pay a reasonable charge for the trips, so they were willing to look the other way.

————

DWAYNE WHEELER PLANNED TO KEEP TRACK OF Bill Bulski's activities and see what he could do about him. To Donna Sue's irritation, he turned down several possible capers to go after that dangerous man.

"Dwayne! Why can't you forget that guy? Surely the day will come when he goes too far and will be arrested."

"It's on my conscience, Donna Sue!" Dwayne said as he paced back and forth in the office. "I scolded a boy about bullying younger kids. He wanted to do it because he was getting beatings at home. It was his way of getting even for his awful life. And it turned out that his dad was beating on his mother too. The guy doesn't need to get away with that."

She knew Dwayne was really set on bringing Bill Bulski to justice. "All right. I can see this means a lot to you. I'll be quiet about it."

Dwayne started his campaign by parking near the Newly Machine Shop about the time Bulski would be getting off work. Dwayne had found out that Bulski's car was a 1940 Chevrolet Sedan, and he could see it from where he was parked without being too obvious.

A short time later, Bulski came out of the shop, scowling for no apparent reason other than a naturally surly personality, got in the car, and drove out of the parking area, heading for his house.

The shamus was a skillful stalker and able to keep out of view of the man's rearview mirror. He followed Bulski to his house and watched him pull into the driveway.

Dwayne went a few more hundred feet, then made a U-turn and stopped beside a mailbox on the curb.

He didn't know how long his prey would stay at home since Bulski's wife and son weren't there to serve as targets for his abuse. If the stakeout lasted more than two hours, Dwayne would drive away and wait for a chance to follow him at another time.

That was what happened. Frustrated by his lack of success, Dwayne gave up for the evening and headed home.

That scenario repeated itself the next day. Finally, after two days of observation, Bulski came out of his house within a half hour of arriving there. He had changed his work clothes and was dressed in a fedora, shirt, and slacks. Dwayne watched him back out of the driveway and turn down the street. The shamus started the Nash and followed.

Bulski got on Pawnee Avenue and went west. He reached Hillside and went north. The next turn was west on Stafford. After two blocks, he pulled up to a small apartment house. Bulski got out of his car and walked up to the building.

Dwayne slid the Nash to the curb half a block away and got out of the car. Trying to look inconspicuous, something he had experience in from all the other capers where he'd had to tail someone, he walked to where Bulski had entered the building. There were four mailboxes next to the entrance door. Dwayne took out his small pad and copied down the names and addresses. Three were men and one had a feminine name.

Dwayne went back to his Nash and waited. Two hours passed with no sign of Bulski leaving, then he drove away and headed for home. When he arrived, Donna Sue was sullen.

"Well? Is your quarry still staying home at night?"

"Nope," Dwayne said. "He went to a small apartment house this evening on Stafford Street. There are four people living there in various flats. Each had a mailbox at the entrance to the building. Three were men and one was a woman."

"All right," Donna Sue said. "Shall we assume that Bulski was calling on the woman?"

"You hit the jackpot. Guys like Bulski who beat their wives—"

"—I know. They have paramours, right?"

"Right. But I got to figure out if he was just calling on a buddy or making goo-goo with a lady. It's still possible he wasn't with a dame."

"What if he is?"

"Then I'll knock on the door and tell her what a two-timing boyfriend she's got. And she will get mad, especially because I'll tell her about what he done to his wife and son, too."

"How are you going to get all that done?" Donna Sue asked.

Dwayne thought a moment and then shook his head. "I don't know."

———

THE FIVE STUDENTS AT THE ACTING AND modeling studio were getting walking instructions. Gwendolyn Haversham had them going around in a circle to the tunes that Claudine Ginnette played on the piano. Sometimes she would change the cadence straight ahead, then suddenly turn them to go the other way. It was similar to the way soldiers drilled.

Another thing Gwendolyn wanted from them was to

have their parents purchase two pairs of gymnastic shirts, shorts, and tennis shoes. Each girl had a hook on the wall to hang the garments. They were dressed in regular clothing when arriving, then changed to sports garb for exercising. At the end of the day's work, they changed back to their street clothing.

Every three days, the training was about makeup and hairdressing. The girls loved it when Claudine did their hair. There was a sink in the small back room. Claudine gave the girls' hair a thorough washing, along with massaging their scalps. Then the little French lady snipped and shaped a hairdo that complimented each girl.

The next treatment was manicures for beauty treatment of their fingernails. The girls' hands were put in bowls of warm water to soften them. Then Claudine used a tool called a pusher to shape the cuticle. After that came the filing and shaping of the free edges of the nails. This was followed by a brief buffing. The next and last operation was having red nail polish carefully applied.

The five girls loved this part of their education.

In between their lessons at the *Hollywood Acting and Modeling Studio*, the girls went to their schools like other students. The word went around East High School, North High School and Saint James Catholic High about what they were doing on Saturdays. The reaction was envy in most cases for the girl students but the boys were not particularly interested. They didn't care about that acting and modeling junk, as they called it.

DONNA SUE WAS PREPARING BREAKFAST ONE morning while Dwayne walked out into the hallway and picked up the daily copy of the *Wichita Eagle* lying there. Then he went back into the apartment.

He opened the newspaper, looked at the front page, and gasped. "Goddammit to hell!"

Donna Sue turned away from the stove. "What's the matter?"

"Look**ie** here!" he said, holding the paper so she could see the headline.

"Oh my god!"

DOUBLE MURDER OF HUSBAND AND WIFE

The victims were Leonard Thompson and his wife Margaret.

CHAPTER 9

Dwayne entered the Wichita Police Department's homicide office. He hurried through the door and walked rapidly toward the desk of Detective Lieutenant Ben Forester. Sergeant Al Gallagher tried to stop him before he could get there. "Where the hell do you think you're going, shamus?"

"Up yours, Gallagher," Dwayne said, continuing to the lieutenant's desk. He and Gallagher had been feuding for several years.

"Hey, Ben," Dwayne said. "Who do you have on that Thompson caper?"

"The same guy you just passed," Forester said, grinning. "Your favorite cop."

"Aw, shit, Ben!"

"I don't have anybody else," the lieutenant said, spreading his hands. "Take him or leave him."

Dwayne walked back to Gallagher's desk. "Ben sent me to you. I got some info on the Thompson couple."

Gallagher, a professional despite his dislike for

Dwayne, turned serious, pulled a pad and pencil over in front of him. "Okay. Tell me what you know."

"The first thing I'll tell you is who did it. The guy's name is William Bulski. Leonard Thompson and I put his sister Dora in the Salvation Army's home for mistreated women. Her son Troy Bulski went with her."

"Mmm," Gallagher mused. "So tell me about this William Bulski."

"He was why we took his wife and kid to the Salvation Army. Bulski beats the crap out of his wife. When Thompson and I went to the Bulski house, she was black and blue."

"Let me get into the photos of wife beaters," Gallagher said. "Wait up."

The sergeant went across the room to several file cabinets. He pulled out a packet and went through it. He found what he was looking for and returned to his desk.

"Here," Gallagher said. "Is this the photo of the Bulski you're talking about?"

"That's him. He must've been in trouble before or you wouldn't have a file on him. Geez, Gallagher, you should've tumbled to this guy already. He shoulda been your prime suspect!"

Gallagher glared and slapped the file down on the desk. "We hadn't uncovered the relationship between him and the victims yet. The killings just happened last night. What do you think we are, Wheeler? Magicians?"

Dwayne took a deep breath, got his anger under control, and put a more conciliatory tone in his voice as he went on, "We can go down to where he works. It's the Newly Machine Shop on George Washington Boulevard."

Seeing Bulski brought to justice was more important than his feud with Gallagher.

The sergeant still glared but seemed willing to call a truce. He stood up and said, "Let's go, shamus."

"After you, Sarge."

The two went to the back of the building and got into a homicide department car. Gallagher drove over to Hillside Avenue then down to George Washington Boulevard. When the Newly Machine Shop came into sight, the sergeant pulled into the parking lot.

The two walked up to the door and went inside the noisy interior. A lady receptionist looked up at them. She recognized Dwayne. "So you're back again."

Gallagher interrupted. "We're here to see William Bulski."

"He hasn't been in for the last three days." The receptionist spoke loudly to be heard over the racket. "I'll buzz the foreman."

Five minutes later, the foreman walked up. He recognized Dwayne. "So you're back again," he remarked, the same as the receptionist. "I take it you're looking for Buski."

"Me and this police sergeant want to find him."

"We don't know where he is. I hope nothing bad happened to him."

"I do," Dwayne said.

Gallagher pulled out a card and gave it to the foreman. "If Bulski shows up, telephone me. And don't tell him that you're calling me."

"Okay, sure," the foreman replied.

"And here's my card," Dwayne said. "You be sure and call me too."

Dwayne and Gallagher walked back to the cop's car. After they got in, Dwayne spoke up. "I think I know where Bulski's girlfriend lives."

"Where at?"

"Drive to Hillside Avenue and go west to Stafford. You'll find a four-unit apartment building."

"Okay. Which unit is she in?"

"I think it's the first one," Dwayne said.

"Don't you know?"

"Well, there's four mailboxes at the entrance. Three of 'em are men and the first is a female. The name was Brenda Howell."

"That must be her, shamus."

They reached Stafford and Gallagher, turned to the west and went down to the apartment building. He came to a stop and the two of them got out. They walked up to the mailbox.

"Brenda Howell, just like I said," Dwayne pointed out.

"Here goes," Gallagher said, rapping on the door.

A meek voice sounded from inside. "Who are you?"

"Wichita Police Department," Gallagher said. "We would like to talk to you, Miss Howell."

At first the door was opened only slightly, then it swung back all the way. Both Dwayne and Gallagher gasped. The woman had a smashed nose, black eyes, and split lips.

"It looks like Bulski has been here," Dwayne said.

"Yes," she answered. "It was Bill. He got mad at me when I wouldn't go with him."

"Go where?" Gallagher asked.

"Bill didn't say. Just that he had to get out of town. Then he suddenly went crazy and started hitting and kicking me. I tried to stop him, but there was nothing I could do."

Dwayne spoke up. "Listen, Brenda, he might be back. We think he's murdered a married couple."

"Oh god!" she wailed. Her eyes rolled up and she fainted.

Dwayne caught her before she hit the floor. He gently laid her down on a nearby sofa.

"I'll go out to the car and call for an ambulance," Gallagher said. "She's really in bad shape." He left the room while Dwayne kept a close watch on the woman. She moaned a couple of times but didn't regain consciousness.

In ten minutes, Gallagher was back. "She'll be taken to the Saint Michael Hospital pronto. We'll wait here then follow the ambulance. I also requested a guard rotation for her room."

Brenda opened her eyes and looked around. "Oh," she said after recalling what was going on.

"You'll be going to the hospital," Gallagher told her. Then she fainted again. Dwayne wasn't sure she understood what Gallagher told her before she passed out the second time.

In fifteen minutes, the ambulance arrived. The driver and doctor put Brenda on a gurney and wheeled her out of the apartment. Dwayne and Gallagher got in the police department car and followed the vehicle.

When they arrived at the hospital, Brenda was taken to a treatment room. A policeman to guard her also showed up. "What's going on?" he asked Gallagher. "I hear they're putting a rotation on us guys to stand a watch."

"She was beaten up by her boyfriend and he might come looking for her," Gallagher said. "The guy's the leading suspect in a double homicide."

The uniformed officer let out a low whistle of surprise at that news.

"Well," Dwayne said. "I'm going to the Salvation

Army's place for beaten women. I'll have to tell Dora that her brother and sister-in-law have been murdered. They won't have heard about it yet."

Gallagher sighed. "Better you than me, Wheeler. I always hate having to do that. Come on, I'll drive you back to your station wagon."

———

DWAYNE WAITED IN A CONFERENCE ROOM FOR Dora at the women's sanctuary. He had informed the Salvation Army lady in charge that he had bad news.

When Dora walked in, she showed a smile seeing Dwayne. Then she realized that he was in a sad way.

"Hello, Mr. Wheeler," she said haltingly.

"I have tragic news," Dwayne said. He knew that trying to ease into it wouldn't do any good. "Your brother Leonard and his wife were murdered a couple of days ago."

"Oh god! No! No!" Dora burst out weeping and took the handkerchief that Dwayne offered her.

"I'm sorry, Dora. But we'll get the killer, don't worry about that."

She looked up with tears running down her cheeks. "It was Bill, wasn't it!"

"Probably. I'm working with the Wichita police to find out."

"I guess...I better go...back and tell Troy...that his uncle Leonard and aunt Margaret..." She stopped speaking and walked out of the room.

Dwayne sat there for a moment to get his emotions under control. He had seen a lot of bad things in his life, but this was one of the worst.

CHAPTER 10

D wayne and Sergeant Al Gallagher went back on the case. Three days after Brenda Howell had been admitted into the Saint Michael Hospital, they were able to visit her. The police guards were still watching over the young woman.

She was sitting up in bed and smiled weakly at the two men as they walked in. Her face still had some bruises on it, but the injuries William Bulski had inflicted on her were healing.

"Here are my knights in shining armor," she remarked. "Thank you ever so much. I'll never forget your kindness."

"We would like to ask you a few questions," Gallagher stated. "We hope you are up to it?"

"Yes, I'll be happy to help you if I can."

"Have you always lived in Wichita?"

"No. I'm from Winfield," Brenda replied. "I decided I wanted to go see what a big city was like." She shook her head. "That was a mistake."

"Where do you work?"

"I'm a telephone operator at the Peavy Commercial Real Estate Office."

Dwayne was getting impatient. As a cop, Gallagher had to go by the book or at least look like he was trying to. But Dwayne was a private detective and didn't have to worry as much about getting everything on the record.

"How did you meet Bill Bulski?" Dwayne asked.

"It was in a tavern," Brenda said. "There were a lot of people mixing up together when I met him. The jukebox was playing and the proprietor didn't mind when a lot of us started dancing. That's how we got acquainted." She paused to take a drink of water from a glass on the bedstand. "I realize now that I was pretty much a hick. He really got to me, I guess."

"Did you know he was married?" Dwayne asked.

"Oh my god! I really didn't know that! I only went out three times with him. When he knocked on my door for the last time, it would be four times. He was acting strangely and wanted us to leave Wichita and go to California. I didn't want to go and he cursed and ranted at me, then suddenly went berserk." She took a breath. "He started hitting me. I was frightened and getting hurt bad. He quit his punching and kicking then suddenly left. When you two knocked on the door, I was scared to death it was him coming back."

Dwayne said, "Well, we'll see that he doesn't."

"You have police protection outside of your door here in the hospital," Gallagher told her.

"Really?"

"Yes, really. When you're ready to leave the hospital, we'll still keep our eyes out for you. And that includes when you go back to your job at that real estate place."

"I won't be going back there," Brenda said. "I'm going back to Winfield."

"That's too bad," Dwayne said. "Wichita is really a nice city."

"You'll never get me to believe that!" she stated. "As soon as I can leave the hospital, I'm gonna call my mother to come get me. Then you won't have to have policemen guard me."

———

GWENDOLYN HAVERSHAM AND CLAUDINE Ginnette had a surprise for the girls after they were dropped off by Mrs. Mary Watson one Saturday. As they entered the *Hollywood Acting and Modeling Studio* they were invited to go to the back room.

When they walked in, they saw Jacques Leroux standing by a projector and screen. There were five chairs in front.

Leroux asked the girls to sit down. "You have been doing so well, that I am going to reward you with some of Hollywood's greatest movies. I am going to show you some delightful films for today's program."

"Where did you get all of those, Mr. Leroux?" Kari Hanson asked.

"I brought them with me from Hollywood."

"What kind are they, Mr. Leroux?" Molly McNally wanted to know.

"They are all musicals!"

Jennie Watson was as excited as the others. "How many do you have?"

"Six," Leroux said. "And we'll tell you the titles one at a time. I shall start number one which is *Wonder Bar*, starring Kay Francis, Dick Powell and Delores Del Rio. *Hollywood Hotel*, also with Dick Powell, Rosemary Lane and Hugh Herbert are second. This will be followed by

Dames. That is yet another Dick Powell also with Ruby Keeler and Joan Blondell. How does that sound?"

The girls answered with happy appreciation.

Leroux continued, "The fourth is *Footlight Parade.* And the stars are once more Dick Powell, Ruby Keeler, Joan Blondell and James Cagney. And the fifth is a very good one too. It is *42nd Street* with Warner Baxter and Bebe Daniels." He paused, then continued with, "And, ladies, we shall end the program with the very, very best. It is *Broadway Melody of 1940,* starring Fred Astaire and Eleanor Powell."

The girls were anxious to get started.

Leroux took out *Wonder Bar* from its case and threaded the film onto the projector's reel. "Here we go!"

The shows began and ran for several hours. Leroux pulled the third film off after it was finished. "Okay, ladies. I understand that Claudine and Gwendolyn have ordered a very delicious lunch from the Continental Grill for you."

"So that's why she told us not to come with sack lunches today," Kari said with a happy smile.

"That is absolutely correct," Leroux said. "You can eat, then come back here for the rest of the motion pictures."

"Aren't you going with us, Mr. Leroux?" Kari asked.

"No, I have some paperwork to attend to. But thank you for the invitation."

The seven females—two adults and five teenagers— left the WKH Building and walked over to North Market Street.

When they arrived at the restaurant, the manager was more than happy to escort the expected young femmes to the back room for lunch.

The meal was fried chicken, mashed potatoes and

gravy, green beans, and dinner rolls. The dessert was apple pie à la mode. During the meal, the girls were so excited talking about the movies that they could be heard by the customers eating out in the dining room.

After stuffing themselves, the group went back to the WKH Building and caught the elevator up to their floor. The girls eagerly sat down and waited as Leroux put on the last two movies *42nd Street* and *Broadway Melody of 1940*.

Those two films ran three and a quarter hours and when the last movie came to a close, the five girls wished there were more.

"Just think, ladies," Leroux told them. "Someday you will be acting and maybe singing in the movies like those you just saw."

It was a dream that made the faces of the girls light up with anticipation and longing. Stardom awaited them. Each and every one of them was convinced of that.

———

DWAYNE AND DONNA SUE ARRIVED AT THE parking garage opposite the WKH Building.

Dwayne braked to a stop in front of the sign that marked their place to park:

WHEELER DETECTIVE AGENCY

He had just switched the engine off when the blast of a gunshot echoed throughout the garage.

Dwayne didn't know where the slug had gone, but he wasn't hit and Donna Sue didn't seem to be, either. He grabbed her arm and pushed her down on the floorboard. He drew his Colt .45 automatic pistol from his coat pocket, threw the station wagon's door open, and got out in a crouch.

The echoes in the low-ceilinged structure made it difficult to be sure where the shot had come from. Dwayne risked a look around the back end of the station wagon and caught sight of the shooter.

It was Bill Bulski. That came as no surprise.

The sound of footsteps could be heard slapping on the concrete pavement as Bulski came toward the station wagon. Dwayne stood up and pulled the trigger on his pistol two times then ducked back down. He didn't think either of his shots had hit their target.

Now Bulski knew where he was and fired three shots. The racket pounded Dwayne's eardrums. Dwayne moved down a car and took a chance at another shot. He fired twice and Bulski yelled.

Dwayne moved carefully in the direction of the howl. He went past a parked car and saw Bulski sitting on the floor, leaning against a pillar. His gun was beside him and blood was coming out of his mouth.

"Don't move!" Dwayne snarled. He pointed the .45 at the man.

"Aw hell, Wheeler...you've done me...a favor..." Bulski looked up and grinned, then slumped down and toppled over to lie in a crumpled heap.

Dwayne didn't lower his gun until he was confident that Bulski was no longer a threat. Then he walked back to the station wagon where Donna Sue waited with a frightened look on her face. All the color had gone out of her features.

"It was Bulski," Dwayne told her. "C'mon and let's call the cops."

"Thank God you're okay," she said.

The couple walked down the ramp to the street and

crossed over to their office. Dwayne dialed the Wichita police homicide department's special number.

"Hello. Sergeant Gallagher speaking."

"Hi, Gallagher," Dwayne said. "Boy, do I have some news for you!"

Chapter 11

Judge William Dodge had called a special conference in his office via a request by Sedgwick County District Attorney Wyatt Cunningham. The other attendees were Dwayne Wheeler, private detective; Sergeant Al Gallagher, Wichita police officer; and Carl Banter, attorney. There was also a court secretary to take notes.

"Okay," Judge Dodge said. "You gentlemen raise your hands."

The three men did as the judge directed.

"Repeat after me. Do you solemnly affirm that the testimony you are about to give will faithfully and truthfully conform to the facts and rules of this conference?"

"I do," they all stated.

"Very well," the judge said. "The Sedgwick County District Attorney has requested that I hold a discussion regarding the death of one William Bulski. I therefore turn our attention to Wyatt Cunningham."

"Thank you, Your Honor," Cunningham said. "About a week ago, a Wichita citizen by the name of

William Bulski was shot dead in a parking garage across from the WKH Building. The killer was one Dwayne Wheeler, a private detective. It appears to me that the late William Bulski was a victim of cold-blooded murder by Wheeler."

Judge Dodge turned to Dwayne. "What have you to say, Mr. Wheeler?"

"I had parked my station wagon in the parking garage across from the WKH Building. Just as I was getting out of my said station wagon, a gunshot was fired my way. I pushed my wife down on the floorboard, then got out of my said station wagon, drawing my United States Army automatic forty-five caliber pistol. A second shot was fired, not only in my direction, but for the purpose of wanting to kill me. I sighted one William Bulski who had deigned to engage me in a gunfight. I, therefore, returned fire and managed to hit William Bulski in the chest with a forty-five caliber bullet. I walked up to him and noted that he was seated against a pillar. I also noted that William Bulski was bleeding from his mouth. Then he said to me, 'Aw hell, Wheeler, you've done me a favor.' Then he grinned and died."

"Mmm, interesting," Cunningham said. "Why would William Bulski want to take your life?"

"Well, Mr. District Attorney, that son of a bitch—"

Cunningham broke in. "Your Honor, I demand that this private detective not insult the man whom he killed."

The judge looked at Dwayne. "Try to be more gentle in your remarks, Mr. Wheeler."

"Yes, Your Honor." Dwayne started again. "Well, Mr. District Attorney, I have to take some time to explain to you why William Bulski wanted to kill me. It started with a schoolboy."

"A schoolboy?" Cunningham said with a sneer.

Dwayne looked up at the judge. "I move that District Attorney Cunningham not interrupt me."

Judge Dodge looked over at Cunningham. "Don't interrupt Mr. Wheeler."

"Thank you, Your Honor," Dwayne said. "So! As I said before being interrupted, this entire situation began with a schoolboy. He showed up at my office one morning, I don't recall the exact date, and told me he was being bullied at Roosevelt Junior High School. The schoolboy, who was a seventh grader by the name of Tommy Carson, wanted me to go put a stop to the bullying. He offered me a dollar, but I told him he didn't have to pay me anything. So I took him over to Roosevelt Junior High School. When we arrived, the schoolboy told me the bully was a ninth grader by the name of Troy Bulski. We went to the principal, a very nice gentleman by the name of John Franklin, and told him of Tommy Carson's problem. The principal had Troy Bulski taken out of his classroom to come to the office. He told Troy Bulski to stop harassing Tommy Carson and to apologize to him. Tommy Carson accepted Troy's apology, and that was that."

"Just a minute!" Cunningham exclaimed. "What does this have to do with you killing William Bulski?"

"Well, he was Troy Bulski's father," Dwayne stated. "So I asked Principal John Franklin if he had any information about Troy Bulski's parents. The principal got a card out of a file cabinet and told me that Troy Bulski's father, name of William Bulski, was employed at the Newby Machine Shop on George Washington Boulevard. I drove over there and met William Bulski and told him about Troy Bulski being a bully. William Bulski told me he would whip Troy, and I said that wasn't necessary since Troy apologized. William Bulski told me to mind my own business. And that was that. I minded my own business."

Cunningham was getting very angry. "I think that Dwayne Wheeler is trying to make up things."

"Mr. District Attorney," the judge said, slamming down his gavel. "I will not have you trying to keep Mr. Wheeler from defending himself." He turned his eyes toward Dwayne. "Carry on, Mr. Wheeler."

"Thank you, Your Honor." Dwayne cleared his throat. "Well, some time passed and a man by the name of Leonard Thompson came into my office and wanted me to protect his sister who, as it turned out, was married to William Bulski. That was Dora Bulski, nee Thompson. He said his sister wanted to divorce William Bulski because he was beating her a lot. I asked him if she had gotten legal papers to make William Bulski leave her alone. Well, that son..." Dwayne paused and grinned. "Sorry, Your Honor, I almost said son of a bitch again."

"By God!" Cunningham yelled. "Your Honor! Wheeler is getting very crude and disrespectful!"

Judge Dodge banged his gavel. "Mr. Wheeler, you *are* getting a bit out of hand."

"I apologize, Your Honor. Anyhow, William Bulski really went crazy to the point that his wife Dora was afraid for her life. I told Leonard Thompson that we should take his sister and her son Troy Bulski to the Salvation Army's place where they can be protected from rotten husbands and fathers." Dwayne paused for a moment, then continued. "Well, a terrible thing happened. Leonard Thompson and his wife Margaret were murdered in their home."

Attorney Carl Banter interrupted. "Your Honor, I believe it is time to dismiss Mr. Wheeler. Sergeant Al Gallagher of homicide can take over."

"Whew," the judge said. "We will take a break for an hour. Then the policeman can be interrogated."

———

DWAYNE, SERGEANT AL GALLAGHER AND Attorney Carl Banter went across the street from the courthouse to a *Kings-X* kiosk hamburger stand for lunch. There was a bench where they could sit down to eat.

Gallagher took a bite of his hamburger and chewed thoughtfully. Finally, he looked at the lawyer Banter. "What the hell is going on with that district attorney?"

"He's a pain in the neck," Banter replied. "One of these days he's going to go too far."

Dwayne took a sip of milkshake. "He got pretty mad at me, huh?"

"Don't worry even if you rattled him," Banter said. "This is just a conference."

They finished their lunch and put the paper wrappings in the nearby wastebasket. "Let's stretch our legs while we can," Gallagher suggested.

"Good idea," Dwayne said.

The trio was silent as they walked around a couple of blocks. After fifteen minutes, they returned to the courthouse. They climbed the stairs to the third floor, where Judge Dodge's office was. When they walked in, they saw the judge and district attorney waiting for them.

"Ah! Here they are," the judge said. "I believe Sedgwick County District Attorney Wyatt Cunningham is ready to question Sergeant Alfred Gallagher." He turned to look at the sergeant. "Remember you're still sworn in."

"Sergeant Gallagher, were you the investigator on the murder of the Thompsons?"

"I was."

"What clues, if any, did you find?"

"Well, we didn't find clues. The only thing we noted was that the husband and wife were lying close together and the entrance to the house was not broken in. There were no fingerprints except the couples' and no bloody footprints."

Cunningham was smirky. "I guess you policemen must have been missing something in that murder house, no?"

"That's true," Gallagher agreed. "However—"

"—however what, Sergeant?"

"However, we had the coroner remove the bullets out of the deceased," Gallagher said. "Then we checked Bulski's bullets that were fired at Dwayne Wheeler. They matched up."

"Uh...they did, huh?" Cunningham stammered.

"Yes," Gallagher said calmly. "And I might say, Mr. District Attorney, that Dwayne Wheeler is a very brave and skillful private detective."

Judge William Dodge grinned. "Well! I guess I might as well call this conference discontinued." He looked over at the court secretary. "Type up the record of this meeting and give me a copy no later than tomorrow."

District Attorney Cunningham sat in his chair with a frown on his face. Dwayne, Gallagher, and Banter walked out into the hall. Banter nodded to his companions. "Well, guys, I'm off to visit a prisoner over in the county jail. He's a breaker-and-enterer."

The lawyer walked away and Gallagher turned to Dwayne. "I want to tell you something, shamus. You're one hell of a good man."

"Well, Sarge, I've begun to like you too."

The two Wichitans shook hands.

CHAPTER 12

It was Caroline's mother's turn to drive the girls to their practice. There were four girls in the back seat while Kari's mother, Borghild Hanson, was sitting with Caroline in the front. The two mothers were planning a shopping spree after the girls were let out at the studio.

Mrs. Taylor stopped in front of the WKH Building and the girls piled out onto the sidewalk. After an elevator ride up to the second floor, they hurried to their acting and modeling lessons.

When they walked through the door, Gwendolyn was waiting for them. "Well! I'm glad you could make it." Her voice held a slight tone of impatience.

Carolyn said, "My mom had to pick up Kari's mom to go shopping."

Molly McNally spied a phonograph sitting on a table. "What's that for, Miss Haversham?"

"Go change into your gym suits and you'll find out. By the way, don't put on your tennis shoes."

"Why not?" Rachel Carlson asked.

"Just do as I say," Gwendolyn said. "And hurry up!"

Ten minutes later, the five girls walked back into the room barefooted. "Now what?" Molly McNally wanted to know.

"Here's 'now what.' You're going to learn Exotic Dancing," Gwendolyn said.

Caroline Taylor asked, "What's Exotic Dancing?"

"I am going to teach you what Exotic Dancing is," Gwendolyn replied. "Now make a semicircle." She waited while they lined up. "Exotic Dancing is done by the movement of hips and torso."

Claudine Ginnette suddenly appeared from another room. She seemed wicked to the girls from the way she was dressed.

"All right, ladies," Gwendolyn said. "Claudine is not only barefooted, she is attired in what is called the proper Exotic Dancing costume. She is wearing the *bedlah* style bra, a hip belt, and harem pants."

Gwendolyn looked over at Claudine. "Put that record on the phonograph."

Claudine put on the record and started the turntable. The music that came out flowed and spiraled and definitely seemed to be exotic to the girls. It sounded like something they would hear in a movie set in Casablanca or the Casbah. The French woman began to dance, and the girls were amazed.

"Okay, Claudine," Gwendolyn said. "Now do *percussive*."

Claudine's hips moved in a staccato pattern that made her hips seem like they had a mind of their own and were detached from the rest of her body.

"Now *fluid*."

Claudine made *sinuous,* a method of flowing movements in a continuous motion.

"Next *shimmy*, Claudine."

She did continuous vibrations with her hips, then made all the movements one after the other, combining and forming what became a fluid, seductive, sensual dance.

The music came to a stop and Claudine quit dancing. All the girls' mouths hung open in amazement at what the French girl had done.

Gwendolyn smiled. "It is like a harem. An Arabian harem. Okay, girls, let us get to it. Line up and spread out!"

Claudine started the phonograph again.

Gwendolyn directed the next motion to do. "Start with the *percussive* and do the staccato with your hips. Keep going back and forth...no, Molly! You're not making enough movement. Go back and forth in a sexy way... Caroline, you're holding your hips in too tight. Make wide back-and-forth movements. Ah! Karli and Jennie, you're doing just fine. Keep it up! Not bad, Rachel. Everybody listen to the music and get in step with it."

The girls continued, adjusting to Gwendolyn's orders for another half hour. Eventually they began growing weary, stumbling and losing their balance.

"Okay," Gwendolyn said. "Sit down and rest. I want to explain something else to you. And that is, you must follow a path to awareness. There are what is called the Six Cauls. The first is the Caul of Dismissal, the second is the Caul of Seeing, the third is the Caul of Worship, the fourth is the Caul of Communion, the fifth is the Caul of Commitment and the sixth is the Caul of Tranquility."

Kari raised her hand. "I'm sorry, Miss Gwendolyn. I don't have the slightest idea of what you're talking about!"

"Me neither," Jennie said.

"Ah hah!" Gwendolyn said. "None of you know of

the Cauls, but as you pass into more Exotic Dancing, they will descend slowly into your covert psyche." The girls looked at each other with a complete lack of understanding.

"All right!" Gwendolyn said. She looked over at Claudine. "Put the record on again."

———

IT WAS TWO O'CLOCK IN THE MORNING WHEN Elmer Pettibone's telephone rang. His wife Jewel heard the third ring and reached over on the bedstand to pick up the receiver.

"Hello?"

"Is that you, Mrs. Pettibone?"

"Yes," she said, irritated. "Who is this?"

"I'm Don MacTavish. I need to talk to Mr. Pettibone. It's important."

Jewel reached over and gave Elmer a good shaking on his shoulder to wake him up. He opened his eyes, then turned over to face her. "Whatcha want?"

"It's Don at the taxi radio system."

Elmer took the receiver. "What's up, Don?"

"Our system just went blank," Don said. "We can't get reception or transmission."

Elmer sat up. "What the hell do you mean?"

"I mean, our radio station is dead."

"Okay. I'll be down there right away."

Elmer got out of bed and reached for his trousers, muttering curses as he pulled them on. Jewel was worried and asked, "What's wrong?"

"Something's haywire with our radio system."

Twenty minutes later, Elmer walked into the station

on top of the Ellis Singleton Building. "What's up? Say something into your mike."

"Hello, hello!" Don said.

Elmer tried it and got nothing broadcasting in or out. "What the hell is going on?"

The nearby telephone rang and Elmer picked it up. "Hello, this is *Speed-O Taxi Service.*"

A man's voice sounded. "Hello, *Speed-O Taxi Service.* Can't you use your radio system?"

"Uh...no, we can't." Elmer frowned. "How'd you know that?"

The man didn't answer directly. Instead, he said, "I know how to fix it."

Elmer was puzzled. "How?"

"By you paying me five thousand dollars."

"What the hell are you talking about?" Elmer asked.

"My organization will turn your system back on if you pay us five thousand dollars," the voice said. "But you must follow our directions."

Elmer's hand clenched on the telephone. "You son of a bitch!"

"Tsk, tsk. That's not friendly. We'll call again. Think about it."

_____

CHAPTER 13

Donna Sue had written up a report on a caper Dwayne had just completed. It involved the amount of money charged in a beauty parlor. It seems that two out of the five operators were not charging the same amount to all the customers. They were giving their personal friends cheaper prices, but still ringing them up like the regular amounts to the parlor's owner. It was difficult to figure out since there were so many styles of treatment from buffing fingernails to dressing hair. But Donna Sue knew *who* was doing *how much* through her knowledge of beauty salons.

The two culprits were fired.

Dwayne was amazed at his wife's abilities. "If it wasn't for you, I would've had to give up that case. Those two little twerps got their comeuppance."

"They sure did," Donna Sue said, pleased that she had been able to help Dwayne on a caper. She had done more than help, she realized. She had actually solved the whole thing. She didn't want any special credit for that, though. She and Dwayne were a team. "Well, I think I'll call the

Reliable Answering Service and see if Millie has any messages for us."

She dialed the number and learned there were no calls for the Wheeler Detective Service.

"Hello, you two."

The unexpected greeting came from the office doorway. Fritz Harrigan stood there with a smile on his face. He had been a schoolmate of Dwayne at East High School. He had also led the way in defeating the schemes of a *Nazi SS* unit destroying the monetary units of the South American nations of Argentina, Bolivia, Chile, Paraguay, and Uruguay. Fritz had shown his skill at engraving engineering.

This was done by engraving money printing plates not only for the *Nazis* but for the countries themselves. The operation was set up in a desolate area of western Kansas, in a building that had served as a training school for code-breakers during World War II. Fritz, tricked by the Nazis into working for them, eventually had been able to turn the tables on them with some help from Dwayne.

"Well, Fritz," Dwayne said. "What've you been up to lately?"

"I've been spending the fortune I got for the money engraving I did." The little guy looked like it, because he was well-dressed and had an air of success about him.

"I bet you've had a lot of fun, didn't you?" Donna Sue said.

"Well, I did a lot of dating, but I didn't find any woman as beautiful as you, Donna Sue."

"Flatterer!"

"I came home to see Mom and the rest of the Harrigan clan."

"So how are—"

"—damn it, Dwayne, you gotta help me!"

The interruption came not from Fritz but from Elmer Pettibone, who yelled out his demand as he pushed past Fritz and rushed into the office.

"Whoa!" Dwayne said, holding up both hands with the palms out in a gesture for Elmer to slow down. "What's the matter?"

"I'll tell you what's the matter! There's somebody who has shut off my radio system. I can't call the taxis and they can't call me. And the bastards who done it said I'd have to pay 'em five thousand dollars if I wanted it turned back on."

"Uh oh!" Fritz said.

Elmer turned toward him. "What the hell do you mean by 'uh oh?'"

"Oh god!"

"What the hell do you mean by 'Oh god.'"

"Well...I have a nephew who is an ace on radio waves," Fritz said. "But I don't think he'd cut off your system for cash. He's only fourteen."

"Oh, yeah?"

"Okay," Dwayne said. "Let's stay cool about this. It'd be a hell of a coincidence if Fritz drops by to say hello and his nephew turns out to be behind your trouble, Elmer."

"You got a better idea?" Elmer asked.

"Well, no, I don't suppose I do." Dwayne turned to Fritz. "Do you have any idea if your nephew would do something like that?"

"I don't know," Fritz admitted. "I've been out of Wichita for a long time. And there are not very many guys who are experts in radio waves or whatever they are."

"I tell you what," Dwayne said. "Let's go over to your nephew's house. It's a place to start, anyway. Where does he live?"

"He lives on Erie Avenue close to East High. His name is Larry Harrigan."

"Let's go," Elmer said.

Donna Sue spoke up. "I'm gonna have to stay here in case of any calls for other capers."

"Okay then," Dwayne said. He snagged his hat off the hat tree just inside the door. "C'mon, we'll go across the street to the parking garage."

The three hurried over to get into Dwayne's station wagon. He backed up then went down the ramp to South Market Street and headed east then south on Erie Avenue.

"There's my aunt and uncle's house," Fritz said a short time later, pointing to one of the residences.

Dwayne pulled up to the curb, then the three men walked onto the porch. Fritz knocked, then called out, "Uncle Ned! Aunt Anne!"

The door was opened by his aunt Anne, a pleasant-looking middle-aged woman. "Hello, Fritz. Who are your friends?"

Fritz ignored the question. "Is Larry here?"

"Yes. Come in."

His uncle was seated in an easy chair reading the *Wichita Eagle*. "What's going on, Fritz?"

"These are friends of mine. We'd like to see Larry."

"Sure. He's up in the attic. You know the way, Fritz."

When the trio climbed up to the attic, they walked into what looked like an electronics factory.

Larry looked up from a workbench at the group. A little curl of smoke rose from the tip of the soldering iron he had been using on a complex circuit board in front of him. "Hi, Fritz."

"Hi, Larry. These are friends of mine and they're interested in your radio waves or whatever they are."

"Sure."

Elmer was stressed looking over the equipment in the attic. "Do you have a radio broadcast wave in all this?"

"Let me handle the boy," Fritz said as he held out a hand and motioned for Elmer to calm down. "Did you cut off this man's taxi radio system and tell him you would turn it back on for five thousand dollars?"

"No," Larry said. "Gee, Uncle Fritz, I wouldn't do a thing like that. But I bet I can tell you who is doing it."

"Who are they?" Elmer asked.

"There's some East High guys I know who have a swell set up of radio wave stuff."

Dwayne stepped in as his detective instincts took over. "What's their names and where do they operate their wave stuff or whatever you call it."

"It's just over a couple of blocks from here," Larry said. He got a notebook and wrote the address on a page, then handed it to Dwayne. "Here's where you can find them. One is Darrell Fenley. He lives there with his folks. The other is Herbert Norton. I don't know where he lives, but he spends a lot of time with Darrell up in his attic."

"How many radio wavers are in Wichita?" Dwayne asked.

"Only me, along with Darrell and Herbert, as far as I know," Larry answered.

Dwayne looked at Elmer. "Well, I'm a private detective with a badge. D'you want to hire me to arrest those two?"

Elmer grinned. "Yeah."

"We've gotta have proof that they're guilty, though."

"Arrest them, then get the proof!"

Dwayne chuckled. "Not a bad way to go about it."

He took a second look at the address of Darrell Fenley.

Fenley lived south of Wichita High School East on Grove Street.

"Let's go," the shamus said. He led the way to his station wagon with Elmer. Fritz decided to stay there with Larry and the boy's parents.

When Dwayne and Elmer reached Fenley's house, they went up on the porch and Elmer hammered on the front door before Dwayne could knock. An angry man answered the summons. "What do you want?"

Dwayne flashed his badge. When you didn't have proof of something, it was usually better to act like you did. That often stampeded suspects into confessing. "I am here to arrest Darrell Fenley on charges of making a felonious threat."

The man was stunned. "Darrell is my son! He would never do such a thing." He turned around and hollered, "Darrell! Get down here!"

There was a clumping from the attic and the youth appeared. "What's wrong?"

"This policeman says you committed some crime or another. What the hell have you been up to, son?"

Dwayne stepped into the house, leaving Elmer on the porch. "Turn around!" he ordered. Darrell hesitated but then gave in to the tone of command. The private eye clapped a pair of his handcuffs on the boy and led him out to the porch. "C'mon!"

Mr. Fenley was stunned. "Have you done something, Darrell?"

"No, Dad!"

Dwayne took Darrell over to the station wagon with Elmer following.

The next stop was to arrest Herbert Norton. Darrell was shaken up enough by being handcuffed that he spilled Herbert's address without any hesitation. The house was close by. Dwayne left Elmer to watch Darrell and went up to the door. This time, he was the one who knocked hard.

A woman answered, her face showing anger at being disturbed. "Who are you and what do you want? If you're selling something—"

Dwayne showed his badge. "I'm not selling anything, lady. I'm here to arrest Herbert Norton."

"Arrest—! For what?"

"For the crime he and Darrell Fenley committed." He turned and pointed at the car. "See?"

The woman saw Darrell sitting in the back seat with a guilty, hangdog expression on his face. She gasped. "What have those boys been doing?"

"You can find out later," Dwayne replied. "Believe me, it will go easier on both of them if they tell the truth and get this thing cleared up."

"Oh my god!" She turned around. "Come out here, Herbie."

The boy appeared. "What is it, Ma?"

"This is a policeman. He said you and Darrell have committed a crime."

Herbert's eyes widened and bugged out from sudden fear. "Oh god! I told Darrell we couldn't get away with it. I told him he was nuts, but he said we'd be rich."

Dwayne knew that was it. The kid was so scared he'd spill his guts about the whole thing.

Herbert saw his buddy sitting in the car, a prisoner. "I'll go," he said meekly. He even stuck his hands out to make it easier for Dwayne to slap the cuffs on him.

Dwayne handcuffed him and took him to the car with a firm hand on his shoulder. Once the two boys were secure in the back seat, Dwayne drove to the Wichita Police Station.

CHAPTER 14

Judge Dorothy Dawson was a forty-five-year-old Sedgwick County jurist, who had never married. Her father, Orville Dawson, was a cowboy who came to Wichita after herding cattle up the Chisholm Trail to the railroad. He settled down in the town as a deputy sheriff and married a local young lady. The couple had five children, the youngest being Dorothy.

All the rest of the Dawson kids were good citizens but Dorothy went a couple of steps farther. She worshipped her pa and wished she was a man and could wear a star on a vest. That was impossible, of course, so she settled down to deal with the law by becoming a lawyer. At first she was ignored, but after she had kept a half dozen men out of jail, it wasn't long before the folks in town found out she was a damned good attorney. Eventually she ran for the position of Sedgwick County judge and was elected to that post.

Now, after twenty years of dealing with the law in one form or another, she was still going strong.

———

DWAYNE WHEELER AND ELMER PETTIBONE WERE seated in the courtroom. They glanced over and saw Darrell Fenley's and Herbert Norton's parents walk in, looking upset, afraid, and angry, all at the same time.

Judge Dorothy Dawson entered from her office and sat down on the bench after the bailiff had called out for everyone to rise. As those in the courtroom settled back into their chairs, the judge nodded down at her secretary Paula Reynolds, then looked over at the prosecution.

"Well, Assistant District Attorney Jane Anderson. How are you today?"

The prosecutor rose to her feet and nodded. "Ready to go, Your Honor."

The judge was always happy to see a female prosecutor. "What have you got?"

"It involves a ransom," District Attorney Jane Anderson answered.

"A kidnapping?"

"No, Your Honor. It has to do with a taxi company."

"Well, this sounds like it's going to be interesting," Judge Dawson said. She looked over at her bailiff Harry Rolf. "Bring in the defendants, Harry."

Harry walked to the side door and opened it. "Okay. C'mon in."

The bailiff ushered in an attorney by the name of Sam Wendall with the prisoners Darrell Fenley and Herbert Norton, who wore their own clothes instead of jail uniforms but looked terrified.

Judge Dawson nodded to her secretary. "What are the charges?"

"Ransom to gain money from a business by a felonious threat."

The judge looked at Attorney Sam Wendall. "How do you plead?"

"Not guilty, Your Honor. We wish to get a bond."

"Who is going to put up a bond if there is to be one?" Judge Dawson said.

"A.J. Kessler sent word he would agree to a bond, Your Honor."

Kessler was one of the leading bail bondsmen in Wichita. Dwayne had worked with him many times in the past, but in this caper, fate had put them on opposite sides for a change.

The judge nodded to District Attorney Jane Anderson. "Are you willing to let the defendants be bonded."

"No, I am not, Your Honor. I feel that despite their youth, they are flight risks. Their parents could send them out of the city to stay with relatives."

Wendell said quickly, "My clients' parents are not wealthy people, Your Honor, and they're law-abiding folks, as well. They wouldn't do such a thing."

"That may very well be true, but I'm going to defer to the prosecution's wishes in this matter," the judge said. "Escort the defendants back to the Country Jail. I will have my secretary arrange a date for the trial." She banged her gavel. "Court dismissed."

――――――

THE FIVE GIRLS PRACTICED THE EXOTIC Dancing as they were instructed, but they found it getting boring. They still could not understand the meanings of the seven cauls.

Gwendolyn went to see Jacques Leroux in his and Claudine's room at the Riverside Hotel. "I am getting worried, Jacques," Gwendolyn said. "They are not doing well in the Exotic Dancing."

"That is bad," the Frenchman said. "That is the most important thing they must learn."

Claudine was uneasy. "It is true, darling Jacques. What can we do?"

Leroux gritted his teeth. "Americans cannot be told what to do. Especially their females." He was thoughtful for ten minutes, and the two women stayed quiet to see what he would decide. "Well...perhaps the girls could be persuaded if their mothers wanted them to follow our instructions to the letter."

"Yes!" Claudine said. "The mothers are desiring to get their daughters in the cinemas."

"Wait!" Gwendolyn cried as an idea occurred to her. "I have heard of the *Prairie Wind Golf and Tennis Club* in the part of Wichita known as Eastborough. If I could arrange a lunch in that affluent part of the city, the mothers, without their daughters or husbands, would be easy to persuade to see things our way."

Leroux made a wide smile. "You are very intelligent, Gwendolyn. I am certain that you are able to make them see our side of this program."

"I shall make a call to this society club."

"Of course," Leroux said.

Claudine felt a stab of jealousy at the way Leroux praised Gwendolyn.

Gwendolyn walked over to the phone on the bedstand. She got the phone book and looked up the number. Then she put her fingers in the rotary dial and spun it.

The director of the club, Jacob Blumberg, answered the phone. "*Prairie Wind Golf and Tennis.* How may I help you?"

"My name is Gwendolyn Haversham. I am the director of the *Hollywood Acting and Modeling Studio* and I would like to hold a ladies' lunch in your restaurant, if I may."

"Oh!" he said, quite pleased. "I've heard about you."

"We are well known in Wichita," Gwendolyn said.

"Well, we certainly will be happy to arrange a lunch in the club. How many would be attending?"

"It would be me, of course, and my assistant. And there would be five ladies whose daughters are being primed for Hollywood. So that would be seven of us."

"What day and time do you require?" Blumberg asked.

"This coming Friday at two o'clock."

When the arrangements were complete, Gwendolyn hung up. "Now we will see how eager I can make the girls' mothers."

———

THE LUNCHEON THAT WAS SERVED IN THE *Prairie Wind Golf and Tennis Club* was the most delicious and exceptional in all of Eastborough. The five ladies were all in first rate spirits. Here were the two women—from Hollywood studios—going to make their wonderful daughters into lovely and wealthy movie stars. After the meal, a tea service was served for the ladies along with different pastries.

When those snacks were completed, Gwendolyn stood up with a big smile. "Well, ladies, I would like to take the time to describe to you how your daughters are getting along. They are doing wonderful overall, but there have been a few slips now and then."

Rachel Carson spoke up. "What sort of slips?"

"Oh! Just little things," Claudine said. "You know, girls will be girls."

"My girl told me about the Exotic Dancing," Margret McNally said.

"Yes," Jenny Watson stated. "I am a bit worried about the word 'exotic.'"

"Goodness," Gwendolyn said. "That word 'exotic' is a Hollywood 'Exotic', and that is a sort of exaggeration in any scene that shows lovers on a dance floor or tap dancing in a musical movie. It is movie slang, actually."

Borghild Hanson chuckled. "That's a relief!"

Claudine smiled and repeated a warning that had been issued before. "I hope you are keeping your daughters away from boys. It would be awful if one lost their purity or, God forbid, became pregnant. The producers would simply turn their backs on her."

"That would be not only a disgrace but also a loss," Gwendolyn told them.

"Why can't we go to Hollywood to see them while they're there?" Carolyn Taylor asked.

"I don't want to insult any of you?" Claudine said. "But you would just get in the way during their screen tests, costume fittings, makeup application, and a hundred other things."

Rachel Carson spoke up. "That's right, ladies. We've got to keep in mind that the movies have a thousand things to do."

"Of course!" Margret McNally said.

"Well!" Gwendolyn said. "I think we must leave this lovely luncheon. Thank you for coming."

She and Claudine watched them leave.

Claudine said, "Well, I think that takes care of our problems. They will make sure the girls cooperate fully with us."

"Yes, but we still must keep them under our management," said Gwendolyn. "There are still so many things that could go wrong..."

CHAPTER 15

Judge Dorothy Dawson entered the courtroom and called for the jury. When the group entered, she sat down and banged her gavel, then nodded to Harry Rolf, the bailiff.

"Hear ye, hear ye! All rise! The Sedgwick County Court is now in session, the honorable Judge Dorothy Dawson presiding. The case against Darrell Fenley and Herbert Norton, who are charged with demanding a ransom to gain money from a business while making a felonious threat."

Judge Dawson looked over at Sam Wendall with the defendants. "Are you ready, counselor?"

"I am, Your Honor."

"Very well. The prosecutor may step forward and proceed."

Jane Anderson, the assistant district attorney in charge of the case, left the prosecution table and said, "Call Elmer Pettibone."

The bailiff went out into the hall and called for Elmer.

He came in and walked up to the witness stand. The secretary Paula Reynolds stood up. "State your name."

"Elmer Pettibone."

"Raise your right hand. Do you solemnly affirm that the testimony you are about to give will faithfully and truthfully conform to the facts and rules of the court?"

"I do."

"You may be seated."

Jane Anderson walked up to Elmer. After establishing his name and the fact that he was the owner of the *Speed-O Taxi Service* for the record, she said, "Your firm uses radio to communicate with your taxicabs, is that correct, Mr. Pettibone?"

"Yes, ma'am. We use radio waves to talk back and forth with the drivers in the cabs. It's very, uh, modern and up to date."

"But this radio communication system was shut down by outside forces?" She gave the date that the radio station went dead.

"That's right. Nothing was getting in or out on that radio wave."

"You were, in fact, threatened that the radio station of your taxi company would be destroyed unless you paid five thousand dollars to the parties responsible for shutting it down. That threat was made by means of a telephone call to your company. Is that right?"

"Yes."

"Are the persons who demanded the ransom in this courtroom?"

"They sure are," Elmer answered. "That's them at the defendant's table."

For a second, Sam Wendall looked like he wanted to stand up and object, but he abandoned the idea, likely knowing that Judge Dawson would overrule his objection.

Prosecutor Anderson continued. "Can you tell us more about when they contacted you, Mr. Pettibone?"

"Well, it was about four weeks ago when I was waked up by my wife and she said that Donald MacTavish wanted to talk to me on the phone. He's my head radio operator, and he told me that our radio wave wasn't working and he couldn't fix it."

"Then what did you do, Mr. Pettibone?"

"I got dressed and went downtown to where my taxi radio wave station was on the top of the Ellis Singleton Building. Donald MacTavish showed me that it wasn't working."

"Then what happened?"

"The phone rang, and I picked it up, and somebody said to me that I could get my radio wave station fixed if I paid him five thousand dollars."

"How did you react to that, Mr. Pettibone?"

"I hired Private Detective Dwayne Wheeler to help me out, but he didn't know nothing about radio waves."

"What occurred next?"

"Well, by golly, there was a feller in Dwayne's office by the name of Fritz Harrigan when I explained what happened. Mr. Harrigan said he had a nephew who had a radio wave setup in the attic of his house. So we went there and saw his nephew who was Larry Harrigan. We asked him if he tried to get five thousand dollars from me. Larry said no but he had a pretty good idea who might've done it. He said Darrell Fenley and Herbert Norton were a couple of East High School kids who were radio nuts like him. He gave us their addresses."

Sam Wendall rose to his feet. "Objection, Your

Honor, to the insult levied against my clients by the witness. My clients are radio enthusiasts, not nuts."

Judge Dawson looked like she was trying not to smile as she said, "I'll sustain that objection, counselor. The witness's characterization of the defendants as nuts will be stricken from the record." She added to Elmer, "Please remember that we're in a court of law, Mr. Pettibone, and try to observe a degree of decorum."

Elmer bobbed his head. "Yes, ma'am, Your Honor. I won't call 'em nuts no more."

"What did you, Dwayne Wheeler, and Fritz Harrigan do after Mr. Harrigan's nephew told you about the defendants?" Jane Anderson inquired.

"We went over to Darrell Fenley's house. The Harrigan kid didn't know where the Norton kid lived. Dwayne Wheeler arrested Darrell Fenley, and we got Herbert Norton's address from him. Then we went and Dwayne arrested him, too. Then we went up into the attic there. Sure enough, we seen their radio wave machine. I couldn't tell you how it works or how they shut down my radio station, but the equipment was there, sure enough. Dwayne Wheeler accused Darrell Benson and Herbert Norton of trying to ransom five thousand dollars from me. They had pretty much admitted it already, but they got stubborn and said they didn't know nothing about any money. Dwayne Wheeler said he didn't believe them, so we went to the Sedgewick County Jail and turned them in, and I told the cops I wanted to press charges against them."

"No further questions," Jane Anderson said.

"Cross-examination, Mr. Wendall?" Judge Dawson asked.

"No questions, Your Honor."

"Miss Anderson?"

Jane Anderson called a police radio expert to the stand. Under questioning, he testified that he had examined the radio equipment found in the attic of the Norton home and that, in his opinion, it was capable of generating a signal strong enough to jam the radios being used by the *Speed-O Taxi Service*. But there was no way for him to be sure that the boys actually had done that, as he admitted when Wendall cross-examined him.

Dwayne took the stand next and repeated what he had heard Herbert Norton say about telling Darrell Fenley they shouldn't do it, as well as Darrell's contention that they would be rich. Wendell objected that that testimony was immaterial and irrelevant, but the judge overruled him.

After Dwayne stepped down, Assistant District Attorney Jane Anderson said, "The prosecution rests, Your Honor."

Judge Dawson looked at the defense table. "Mr. Wendall?"

Sam Wendall got up from his chair and spoke to the judge. "I would like to call Darrell Fenley, Your Honor."

Darrell walked up to the witness chair. The secretary Paul Reynolds stood up. "State your name."

"Darrell Fenley." The young man looked pale and nervous but relatively composed.

"Raise your right hand. Do you solemnly affirm that the testimony you are about to give will faithfully and truthfully conform to the facts and rules of the court?"

"I do."

"You may be seated."

"Hello, Darrell," Sam Wendall said.

"Hello, Mr. Wendall."

"You heard Mr. Pettibone's testimony, didn't you?"

"Yes, sir."

"Now tell me," Wendall said. "Did you and Herbert Norton *really* want to get five thousand dollars from Mr. Pettibone?"

"No, sir. It was just a joke we wanted to do."

"You two fellows were just messing around with your radio stuff, right?"

"Right."

"What about you telling Herbert that you would be rich?"

"I said we could get rich if we actually went through with it. I never meant that's what we would do. He just misunderstood me, is all."

Wendall nodded solemnly. "Things just sort of got out of hand after that, didn't they?"

"They sure did. We just got carried away. We never meant to do anything wrong."

Wendall looked up at the judge. "I'm finished with Darrell, Your Honor."

"All right, Mr. Wendall." She looked at Jane Anderson. "Do you have any questions?"

"No, Your Honor."

"You can step down," the judge said to Darrell. "Do you have any more questions, Mr. Wendall?"

"Yes. I would like Herbert Norton to take the stand."

Herbert walked up to the witness chair. The secretary Paula Reynolds stood up. "State your name."

"Herbert Norton."

"Raise your right hand. Do you solemnly affirm that the testimony you are about to give will faithfully and truthfully conform to the facts and rules of the court?"

"I do."

"You may be seated."

"Hello, Herbert," Sam Wendall said. "You heard what your buddy said, right?"

"Yes, sir."

"You and Darrell did not have the simplest idea to really get five thousand dollars from Mr. Pettibone, did you? It was all just a joke? Just playing around with your radio and getting carried away?"

Jane Anderson stood up and said, "Who's testifying here, Your Honor, the defendant or his attorney?"

"You've made your point, Mr. Wendall," Judge Dawson said. "Let the defendant go ahead and answer."

"O'course, it was just a joke," Herbert said. "We're just a couple of guys who like radios. We're not criminals."

Wendall smiled. "I'm finished with Herbert, Your Honor."

Judge Dawson looked over at District Attorney Anderson. "Do you have any questions for Herbert Norton?"

She shook her head. "Not a one."

The foreman of the jury stood up. "Judge?"

"Yes?"

"We would like to take a vote now."

"All right," Judge Dawson said. "But you must go back to your jury room."

"Yes, Your Honor."

Everyone in the courtroom was puzzled. This was highly irregular, but Judge Dawson allowed the jury to withdraw for its deliberations and vote. Conversation buzzed in the courtroom for about fifteen minutes, then the jury came out and sat down.

Judge Dawson had gone to her chambers. She returned to the courtroom, and when court was called to order again, she asked, "Have you reached a verdict, foreman?"

He stood up, holding a piece of paper. "Here it is in my hands, Your Honor."

"Very well," the judge said. "Bailiff Rolf, get the verdict and bring it over to me."

"Yes, Your Honor." He took it to the judge.

Judge Dawson looked at the jury foreman. "Is this one hundred percent the verdict? You're all in agreement?"

"Yes, Your Honor."

"Very well." She looked at Darrell and Herbert. "Defendants, please rise."

The boys got to their feet with their lawyer standing beside them.

"Guilty," the judge announced. "Schedule the sentencing hearing, Paula."

CHAPTER 16

When the five young ladies showed up at the *Hollywood Acting and Modeling Studio* one morning they were surprised to see the French gentleman Jacques Leroux with Gwendolyn Haversham and Claudine Ginnette waiting for them. The trio all had worried expressions on their faces.

Gwendolyn waited for the girls to sit down on chairs arranged in a semi-circle. She cleared her throat. "Young ladies, Mr. Leroux has just returned from a conference with the owners of five Hollywood movie studios. And I am afraid he brings us bad news." She sighed and turned to Leroux. "Give the girls your report."

"Thank you," Leroux said. "This *Hollywood Acting and Modeling Studio* is the only one in the entire United States. I know you are unaware of that. I must now inform you that this has been a test to see if other studios such as these could bring out the American girls with the best talents. The movie makers are not satisfied with what has been going on here in Wichita. Their main problem is the difficulty all of you have had with the Exotic Dancing."

Claudine, with tears in her eyes, looked over at Gwendolyn. "I have done my best, Miss Gwendolyn!"

"I know you have, Claudine."

Leroux continued. "There is a fault! A fault right here in Wichita, USA, and it is you girls! I was ashamed at the studio conference when I made my report. They took a vote on whether to continue with the *Hollywood Acting and Modeling Studios* or not. The outcome was three to two to maintain the program. I can tell you I was relieved. But I can also tell you that if another vote is taken it will be five to zero." He paused, then glanced over at Gwendolyn. "It is going to be you, *you*, to save this cinema program!"

He strode across the room and out the door.

Gwendolyn gazed at the girls. "Well, well, well. What are we going to do?"

Kari Hanson spoke up. "We'll work harder, Miss Gwendolyn!"

"Of course we will!" Jennie Watson said. "Won't we, girls?"

Molly, Rachel, and Carolyn cried out a tearful agreement.

Gwendolyn mustered up a smile. "Very well. All we can do is try."

———

SEVERAL PEOPLE SAT IN THE COURTROOM'S spectator area. There was Dwayne and Donna Sue Wheeler, Elmer and Jewel Pettibone, Mr. and Mrs. Lawrence Benson and Mr. and Mrs. Sam Norton. There was also three elderly retirees whose hobby was watching trials in the courthouse.

Judge Dorothy Dawson entered her courtroom and sat down on the bench. She looked over at the prisoners, Darrell Fenley and Herbert Norton, who were wearing jail uniforms this time. Their lawyer, Sam Wendall, stood with them.

The judge said, "Well, here we are. Two youngsters who did a stupid thing. That ended up with your radio equipment being confiscated. Your parents are going to have to pay a very expensive penalty because of the loss of money by the *Speed-O Taxi Service*. The business was not able to operate for seventy-two hours. You said, in court, that you were just playing a joke. Perhaps you were. But you did demand five thousand dollars. And that's what the jury considered. Therefore, they found you guilty of a serious crime. You are both eighteen years old. That makes you adults in the eyes of the law." She looked at Sam Wendall. "Do you have anything to say, counselor?"

"Yes, Your Honor. The boys have done a bad thing, but they've learned their lesson. In a month or so, they will graduate from high school. Both have parents who can afford to send them to a university where they will receive educations that can help not only their future lives, but the commerce in American society. That is that, Your Honor."

"*That* is too bad. I am sentencing Darrell Fenley and Herbert Norton to five years in the State Penitentiary in Lansing. If you practice good conduct, you may get out in three years." She banged her gravel. "Court dismissed."

The Wheelers and Pettibones left the courtroom while the Bensons and Nortons tearfully watched their sons being taken away by two bailiffs.

JACQUES LEROUX'S ANGER AND THE SADNESS OF Gwendolyn Haversham and Claudine Ginnette had shaken the five girls into tears of their own. All of them were determined that they would conquer the Cauls that were so important in Exotic Dancing.

Gwendolyn and Claudine were happily surprised at their charges' determination. The pair also emphasized that the movie studios, far from Wichita, would be pleased with the change of the girls' attitude.

The best dancers were Kari Hanson and Jennie Watson. They were slowly but surely beginning to follow the path to awareness without realizing it. The pair set examples for Molly McNally, Caroline Taylor, and Rachel Carlson.

And they came closer and closer to achieving the goals that had brought Gwendolyn, Claudine, and Jacques Leroux to Wichita in the first place.

CHAPTER 17

The spring of 1948 edged into Wichita, Kansas, in a calm way. The cold of winter wasn't quite over but the weather let up a bit to allow a little warmth for the season.

One happy event for some of the Wichitans was the graduation of the three high schools. There was Wichita High School East, Motto *Go Blue Aces*; Wichita High School North, Motto *Go Redskins*; and Saint James Catholic High School, Motto *Go Shamrocks*.

Among those students were Kari Hanson, Jennie Watson, Molly McNally, Caroline Taylor, and Rachel Carlson. They all were happy about graduation but happier about going to Hollywood to become movie stars.

———

THE HOLLYWOOD ACTING AND MODELING *Studio* was closed. It was time to pack up and head for California. The take-off time was four p.m. The five girls couldn't wait to become movie stars as their parents drove out to the Wichita Municipal Airport for the trip to gaiety and glory.

When the small caravan pulled up to the parking area, the fathers carried their daughter's suitcases as they walked out on the tarmac. Jacques Leroux had his Beechcraft 18 aircraft ready for the trip.

Its motors were chugging along to warm up and the map to the destination was on Leroux's map. Gwendolyn Haversham and Claudine Ginnette were already on board. They looked out the windows at the girls and their parents. Leroux gave the families fifteen minutes to say their goodbyes, then he announced it was time to take off. The girls hurried over to him, and he helped them into the airplane. Then he turned toward the families and waved.

Leroux got onto the plane and entered the cockpit. He began to ease the aircraft over to the runway. After braking, he pulled the throttle out and started to roll, gaining speed until he was airborne.

The families watched the airplane take to the air, then it grew fainter to see in the distance. The girls' fathers gritted their teeth while their wives wept.

———

THE ROAR OF THE ENGINES MADE IT DIFFICULT to hear. Gwendolyn and Claudine looked back at the girls to make sure they were okay. Not one of them, except for Kari, had ever flown in an airplane before.

Claudine had brought along some soft drinks, sandwiches, and candy bars. After two hours of flight, she got up and passed out the goodies. She was glad to see none of the girls were airsick. The toilet was in the rear of the fuselage if nature called. The little French girl took some eats to their pilot Leroux.

The darkness of night was growing and finally the blinking lights of towns below were all that could be seen. Up in the cockpit, Leroux had the autopilot turned on. He had plenty of hot coffee in three thermoses to keep him awake for the rest of this long flight.

———

THE DAWN SLOWLY BRIGHTENED UNTIL IT WAS daylight. The passengers, including Gwendolyn and Claudine, gradually came awake. They all stretched, and Gwendolyn went up to the cockpit.

"How are things going?" she asked Leroux.

"Okay."

"How far to Marpoco?"

"We'll be landing in another hour and a half."

CHAPTER 18

Jacques Leroux landed the Beechcraft and taxied up to the aircraft parking area. The expected bus was waiting for them. Gwendolyn walked down the aisle of seats and woke up the girls.

"We've landed," she said. "There's a bus to take you and Claudine to your final destination. Okay?"

Carolyn Taylor asked, "Aren't you going with us, Miss Gwendolyn?"

"Not now. I have some business to take care of elsewhere."

"Okay!" Kari said. "C'mon, girls! Let's go stand in front of the cameras."

The girls followed Claudine and stepped down from the plane and looked at a bus that appeared streamlined and comfortable.

"Come on," Claudine said. "Follow me!"

The Wichita girls were amazed when they saw their transportation. It was a sleek bus that was lustrous in its decoration. Even the driver was in a fancy uniform. Claudine led the girls aboard and after they all had taken seats, the chauffeur started the motor. He put the vehicle in gear and drove out of the airport.

"Look at all those Mexicans," Molly McNally said as the bus traveled along a street with businesses on both sides and a great many people on the sidewalks.

Rachel Carlson wasn't bothered. "Aw, this is probably a suburb of Los Angeles. I read where there are lots of Mexicans living in California."

They rolled through the town and the girls looked out the bus's windows at the signs on the shops they passed. Molly McNally remarked, "Everything here is in Spanish."

From the front seat where she had been listening to the girls' conversation, Claudine laughed. "You will get used to it."

After the bus reached the end of the town, its speed increased as it traveled along a macadam road. Once more, the girls were amazed. They spied a sign that read:

CARRETERA 8

Claudine Ginnette said, "That means 'Highway Eight.' And, like I said, you will get used to your new surroundings."

The plant life along the route was desert brush. The Kansas girls, used to lush vegetation and wheat fields, thought it ugly. Then Kari Hanson said, "Lookie there! Cactus!"

"We are in a desert," Claudine said. "A few more miles and we will start going up to higher land. It is cooler and there are beautiful blooming plants."

For the next half hour, everyone on the bus was quiet. Then the bus slowed, and the driver turned onto a different road. Now the group was surprised that this new route was leading up into mountains.

Once more, the Kansas girls, used to flat wheat fields, were amazed at their new environment.

———

THE ROAD GREW STEEPER AND THE DRIVER shifted into a lower gear. The growling sound went on for fifteen minutes, then suddenly the driver shifted once more, this time back into the highest gear.

He went around a bend and suddenly a high wall with a door in it came into view. "All right, girls," Claudine said. "We are here."

"What is 'here?'" Kari asked.

"It is a hacienda. That is a Mexican structure with very high walls. You will be amazed by what you see when we enter it."

The girls looked through the front windows of the bus and noted a man wearing a pistol and holster. He was standing by a high thick wooden portal and turned to push it open. The driver drove through into the compound.

There were cabins and bungalows along three sides of the wall and on the farthest was what looked like a mansion. It occupied the entire back of the structure. The bus driver drove up to it and came to a stop at the door.

Claudine Ginnette stood up. "We are to get off the bus now, girls, and we must bring our suitcases with us."

After they disembarked, the bus driver drove away to another part of the wall. A massive wooden door in the mansion opened, and a woman stepped out. She wasn't exactly young but there was something noble and beautiful about her. She gazed at the five girls, then nodded to Claudine.

The little French lady spoke up, "Ladies, I have the

honor of introducing to you Madam Ekaterina Lobanova."

"I am happy to see you have here arrived in being safe. You can settle down for to rest of yourselves and I will be talking at you tomorrow." Madam Ekaterina's accent was heavy but understood. She turned and walked back inside the mansion.

Claudine nodded her head at the girls. "Come with me now. I will show you where you and I will live while we are here."

She led them over to a large bungalow and opened the door for them. "There are several rooms in here. We shall have a big bedroom where we will all sleep on beds, of course. And we will have a dining room where we will be served meals. There is also be a living room and a bathroom."

They walked in and went to the bedroom with six beds. Kari Hanson put her suitcase on a bed, then turned to Claudine. "Tell me something. What does all of this have to do with movies?"

Claudine smiled. "You find out from Madam Ekatrina Lobanova tomorrow."

Once more, the Kansas girls were amazed at their new environment. They cast puzzled and a little bit nervous glances at each other, but for the moment, there was nothing else they could do except cooperate.

In each one of them, though, it was beginning to sink in just how truly far from home they were.

CHAPTER 19

The five girls spent the rest of their first day lounging around with Claudine. Their bathrooms consisted of three toilets with screens around them, six sinks with mirrors over them and four showers. There was also a parquet floor for dancing practice.

The meals served to them were delicious. The first lunch was brought in following a knock on the door. Six meals were on a food cart being pushed by a Mexican boy. The man who followed him was an Arab chef. He watched the table being set while the diners settled down.

"You are liking it?" he asked in an Algerian accent after the girls began to eat.

"Oh, yes!" Molly McNally said.

The chef was happy. "In Algeria I was cook in French Foreign Legion kitchen and learn many recipes. There many soldiers from many nations and I hear you are English. So I always will cook English dishes for you."

Carolyn Taylor said, "We're not—"

Claudine interrupted her. "We will be most happy to eat your English meals."

"I am called Ahab. I thank you for to like my cook."
He walked out smiling.

Claudine looked over at Carolyn. "Be careful when
you speak to some of these people. If you would have told
him that you were not English but American, it would
embarrass him."

"Sorry about that," Carolyn said.

Meanwhile the Mexican youth stood off to one side,
waiting for the women to finish the meal.

————

MADAM EKATRINA LOBANOVA ARRIVED AT TWO
in the afternoon. She was escorted by a large, tough-
looking Slovak man. They were accompanied by a thin
fellow named Benito Dibabu. He was dressed in a straw
Panama hat, a worn suit, and sandals. He carried an old-
fashioned camera that had movable legs, and he also toted
a satchel of photo plates.

Dibabu picked up his equipment and walked over to
the window by the door. He set up the camera on its three
legs and pulled out a plate from the satchel. With practiced efficiency, he inserted the plate into the camera. With
that done, he looked over at the American girls. He
pointed to Carolyn Taylor and snapped his fingers,
gesturing for her to go stand in the window.

She did what he wanted, and he took her picture.
Then he snapped his fingers four more times and all the
girls were photographed. With that done, he left the
cabin.

Madam Ekatrina Lobanova smiled at the girls and
nodded toward her bodyguard. "He Polish. His name
Emeryk."

Rachel Carlson smiled at him. "Hello, Emeryk."

The man's facial features remained immobile.

Madam Lobanova whispered in Emeryk's ear, and he walked over and pulled out a chair from the table. She sat down on it, then looked at the girls.

"I want say for you something," she began. "There camera near to make *plenka cartina*...wait, I should say 'picture show.' You five to be in it." She looked over at Claudine. "Does girls know *tanets*...I am meaning to say dance."

Claudine gave a positive nod. "Yes. But they must exercise the movements to keep up their skill."

"You make practice," Madam Lobanova reminded her. She looked at Emeryk. "Now we go."

Claudine looked over at the girls. "Stand up and curtsey. The **m**adam must be treated politely and humbly at all times."

The girls did as they were told.

CHAPTER 20

The five girls were informally dressed in their gym suits and tennis shoes as they ate breakfast. The door opened and Claudine Ginnette entered their bungalow with Gwendolyn Haversham behind her.

Claudine announced, "Look who I have brought with me."

The girls looked up and grinned to welcome the English woman. Kari Hanson took a sip of coffee. "Welcome to our happy house, friend."

"Thank you," Gwendolyn said. "We shall wait for you in the dance room until you've eaten your fill. I have some important announcements to make." She looked over at the Arab chef. "Ah! Hello, Ahab. I see you are still an excellent cook."

"A thousand thanks," Ahab said with a bow.

The girls took fifteen more minutes to finish their breakfast. Ahab's Mexican servant boy began to clear off the table as the diners got up and headed for the dance room.

They entered the chamber and Gwendolyn gestured

for them to sit down on the bench along the wall. "I have several announcements to make."

Molly McNally raised her hand. "Are we going to go to a movie studio?"

Gwendolyn frowned. "Do not interrupt me!"

"Oh, dear," Molly said. "Sorry!"

"Very well. I am now working under Madam Lobanova. She is busy with other programs." She took a breath and continued. "You do not know where you are, but it is time that I told you. This hacienda is in the mountains of northeast Mexico. You are not in Hollywood, Los Angeles or any other part of California."

The girls looked at each other, then turned their shocked attention back to Gwendolyn.

"You are not going to be in any movies," Gwendolyn continued. "You are going to be Exotic Dancers. This will be done in the presence of groups of extremely wealthy Arabian men. They adore beautiful white women with blond and red hair, particularly virgins. You five will be shown here in the dance room for several visiting Arabians. They are going to bid on you. They all are millionaires."

Kari quickly stood up. "What are you talking about?"

"Darling Kari," Gwendolyn said as a predatory look came over her face, making it look much less attractive. "Are you aware of the term white slaves? Well, that is what you girls are. White slaves to be sold." She smiled. "Madam Lobanova believes as much as a half-million American dollars will be bid by some extremely rich Arab who has many oil fields in his country."

The front door of the bungalow could be heard opening. The scuffle of feet across the floor followed.

"Do you hear that?" Gwendolyn asked. "That is your property being taken away. Everything! You will wear what you have on now. Your new clothing will be exotic costumes. And many times, you will dance naked."

The girls were all on their feet now. Molly McNally's Irish temper flashed. "You're not going to do that to us!"

"Tut tut, Molly. You and your little friends here will be paraded across this very dance floor to be viewed like a cattle auction in Kansas. Our auction of you will result in your hymen being broken by an Arabian. A very wealthy Arabian." She turned and gestured to Claudine. "You may address your charges."

The French woman stood up. "I will spend most days and nights in this bungalow. I warn you not to go on hunger strikes. That is not a good idea. You will be fed by tubes being forced down your throats with soup poured through funnels."

Jennie Watson said. "You and Gwendolyn are forgetting one thing. The letters you sent yesterday for us will reach our families in Wichita."

"Jennie, Jennie!" Claudine said with a sneer. "I threw those letters in a wastepaper basket." She shook her head. "Your families will never see or hear from you again."

There were fearful sobs among the girls.

Claudine growled at them. "Go put on your dance costumes, and I do not want to be talked back at. You are no better than sheep now. I will make you dance until you fall from exhaustion. So obey me always."

CHAPTER 21

It was an early morning when five men impatiently waited for Dwayne and Donna Sue Wheeler to show up at their office. These gentlemen were Dennis McNally, Oskar Hanson, Stanley Watson, Marvin Carlson, and George Taylor. They paced back and forth in the second-story hallway of the WKH Building.

Dwayne and Donna Sue stepped off the elevator and immediately took notice of the agitated men. "Hello," Dwayne greeted them. "You fellas look like you've been waiting for us?"

"Yes," Dennis McNally said. "And we're anxious to hire you."

"Okay." Dwayne unlocked the door and let Donna Sue enter ahead of him. He turned around to the five men. "Come ahead, gentleman. My desk is the second one. I have enough chairs, but they are the folding types."

"We don't care about that, Mr. Wheeler," George Taylor said. "You are Mr. Wheeler, aren't you?"

"You bet. This is my wife and secretary, Donna Sue. Have a seat, gents."

The visitors followed Dwayne's directions. He put his hat on the rack and sat down behind the desk. "Now! What can I do for you?"

"Our daughters are the ones that the *Hollywood Acting and Modeling Studio* promised to make movie stars," McNally said. "But if you look across the hall, you'll see that the rooms there have been cleaned out. The building's manager says they left a debt of a couple of thousand dollars. So that means they won't be coming back."

Watson said, "The most worrisome thing is that we saw them fly away with our girls. That was six weeks back. And we haven't heard a word from our daughters since then."

"I thought being ruled by the Nazis was bad," Oskar Hanson said, "but this situation is worse."

"We want to hire you to find them," Taylor said.

Dwayne looked across the desk at the men. He saw the anger on their faces, but he saw the fear in their eyes, too.

"I'll take the caper," Dwayne said.

"What the hell is a 'caper'?" Carlson asked.

"That's just detective talk for job," Dwayne said. He called out, "Donna Sue."

She appeared in the open doorway. "Yes?"

"The girls that were in that *Hollywood* thing across the hall have disappeared. These are their dads and they want them found. This is a caper for both you *and* me."

"I'm ready," Donna Sue said.

"I have a suggestion where you can start," Dennis McNally said. "You're going to have to go to Hollywood. When we realized the girls had disappeared, I made some calls to studios and explained our predicament. I found them sympathetic and kind. They have spokesmen to answer questions and give advice about youngsters wanting to be in the movies." He reached into the inner pocket of his coat. "There are eight studios. Metro-Goldwyn-Mayer, Paramount, Warner Brothers, Twentieth Century Fox, RKO Productions, Columbia, Universal, and United Artists. They will be waiting for you to visit them."

Dwayne nodded and took the list that McNally held out to him. "You made it easy for me."

"I've read about you in the newspapers, Mr. Wheeler," McNally said. "And I know that if there's anyone to take on this hellish situation, it would be you."

"My wife will be going with me."

"That's fine."

Watson spoke up. "What will the cost be?"

Dwayne looked at Donna Sue. "Answer the man, darling."

"I have to go to my desk to do some figuring, but I'll be back in a jiffy."

Silence settled over the men. They were miserable, scared and mad as hell. A couple of them got up and walked nervously around the office.

Dwayne watched them, feeling the hell they must be going through. He and Donna Sue didn't have any kids, but he could imagine what a nightmare it would be if one went missing.

And these men each had a daughter who seemed to have dropped off the face of the earth.

Donna Sue came back with a typed list and handed it to Dwayne who then handed it to McNally.

10 days skill and know-how @ $10 = $100
10 nights in hotel @ $7 per night = $70
10 days car rental @ $8 per day = $80
Round-Trip Air travel = $500

TOTAL = $750

McNally looked at Dwayne. "Aren't you going to charge for food?"

"Nope," the shamus answered. "We'd be eating anyway, no matter where we are. Unexpected expenses could change the final amount some, but this will do for a start."

"Well," Hanson said. "At least all of the five families here can afford to take on this horrible situation. I can remember in Norway how poor fishermen worried about their sons who had crossed over the Norwegian Sea to join the British Armed Forces."

"Thank you," McNally said. "We—"

"—forget it," Dwayne said as he saw how choked up the man was getting. "Donna Sue and I are more than happy to see what we can do."

Donna Sue smiled. "I'll call up the Air Terminal Building for tickets."

———

THE BUNGALOW WAS TENSE. NOW WHEN AHAB and his Mexican boy came in it was forbidden for the girls to speak to them. Claudine had issued that order. However, the food was still good and nutritious so that the girls would not lose weight and would have plenty of strength to dance.

The girls had only been allowed to keep their gym outfits and tennis shoes. Little Claudine Ginnette had become hell-on-earth. She informed her charges that their Exotic Dancing costumes had arrived.

When the girls looked at them, any courage they might have faded away. The garments had nothing that covered them. There was the bedlah bra, hip belts, and harem pants and skirt. None of it would do much to hide their naked bodies.

"Put them on!" Claudine barked the order like a drill sergeant in the Army.

Kari was angry. "When you wore your Exotic Dancing costume, you were covered."

Claudine laughed wickedly. "Of course I was covered! I wasn't going to dance in front of Arabian oil men, was I? I also would never be naked in front of those men from the Middle East like you are going to be doing." She screamed, "*Now take off those gym clothes and get on those costumes!*"

The girls, whose brassieres and panties had been taken away, undressed slowly.

"*Hurry up, you stupid farmer girls!*" Claudine shrieked. When they all were wearing their costumes, she fastened bands of small bells around their wrists and ankles. "You have your breasts covered up too much, Rachel. Carolyn, lower your harem pants. You're not showing your navel."

She looked them over and finally seemed to be satisfied.

"Take the costumes off and take care of them. If anything happens to them, you will regret it."

The girls weren't sure how they could regret the situation in which they found themselves any more than they already did, but they didn't want to find out how, either.

————

THE FIVE SETS OF PARENTS CAME DOWN TO THE Wichita Municipal Airport to see Dwayne and Donna Sue off. The McNally family and the Hanson family had brought everyone in two cars. They all gathered together to bid the pair goodbye and good luck.

Dwayne and Donna Sue would fly in a Central Airline C-47 that would land in Phoenix, Arizona to take on more fuel to get the rest of the way to the Los Angeles Airport.

"Well," Dwayne said. "It looks like they're pushing out the boarding ramp."

He and Donna Sue made their goodbyes. Dwayne shook hands with the fathers, and Donna Sue gave reassuring hugs to the worried mothers. They hurried across the tarmac to get aboard the plane. After getting to their seats, the couple took one last look through the window at the families, who were huddled together with the men holding an arm around the wives' shoulders. Dwayne gave them the thumbs-up sign.

Chapter 22

After Dwayne and Donna Sue's airplane landed, they hurried through the Los Angeles Airport to the auto-rental area. They were delighted to get a brand new 1948 Ford Sedan. Dwayne asked for a map of the city that would take them to the Hotel Floras Lindas.

The clerk, noting the way the couple were dressed and speaking and taking them for Midwestern tourists, made an offering. "Would you also like a map to the studios too? They're free."

"We sure would," Dwayne said. "Thanks, buddy."

The drive through the city was enjoyable for the Wichita couple. "Maybe we'll see a movie star," Dwayne said.

"I doubt it," Donna remarked. "This doesn't look like a place where one would walk through."

When they reached their destination, Dwayne pulled into the hotel parking area. Dwayne turned off the ignition, and they walked into the lobby.

"Hello," the desk clerk greeted.

"We're the Wheelers," Dwayne said.

"Ah, yes. Your room is ready for you."

Donna Sue was curious. "What does the name of this hotel mean?"

"It means Pretty Flowers in Spanish."

"That's nice," she complimented him. She looked around. "Where are they?"

"There isn't any," the clerk admitted. "But like you said, it's a nice name."

"I guess a lot of stuff in this town is just for show," Dwayne commented.

Dwayne signed the register and got the key to their room on the third floor. A bellboy took the key and their suitcases. He walked them over to the elevator. "Where are you folks from?"

"Wichita, Kansas," Dwayne said.

"You got cowboys there, right?"

"We got cowboys, wrong," Dwayne said. "You've seen too many Western movies. We're an airplane manufacturing city."

"No kidding?"

"The last of the cowboys moved on from Wichita sixty or seventy years ago."

"Well, whaddya know about that? I always thought that if something was in the movies, a guy could believe in it." The bellboy shook his head as the elevator ascended. "You're ruining my illusions, mister."

The elevator reached the third floor, and they were taken to room 304. The bellboy opened the door and handed the key to Dwayne. Dwayne handed the kid a half-dollar coin for a tip.

The bellboy smiled a thank you. "If you need anything, ring us down at the desk. We can get you anything you need. Welcome to the Floras Lindas Hotel."

"Thank you," Donna Sue said.

The bellboy left and Dwayne said, "Well! Well! Let me see that map of the studios."

"It'll be handy," Donna Sue said. "Let's unpack and see where we have to go tomorrow."

———

THE COUPLE ATE THEIR BREAKFAST IN THE CAFÉ next door to the hotel. When they were finished, Dwayne said, "Here goes!"

They walked over to the parking lot and got into the rented Ford sedan. "Hollywood studios, here we come!"

Donna Sue looked at the map. "It shows Metro-Gold-wyn-Mayer is the nearest."

Donna Sue called out the streets until they found the entrance. Dwayne pulled in and came to a halt. There was a gate with the studio's name over it in fancy metal letters, and down at the end was the famous M-G-M lion. A guard came out of his hut.

"What can I do for you folks?"

Dwayne answered, "My name is Wheeler. I was told I could visit the spokesman here. My name ought to be on a list."

"Wait up." The man went back into the hut and checked a roster on a clipboard. He came back. "Are you the detective, Dwayne Wheeler?"

"Yes, I am."

"Okay. Drive down to that nearby building and park."

Dwayne followed his directions. He and Donna Sue got out of the car and walked up the steps to a front door. A young woman was sitting at a desk. "May I help you?"

"Yes, you can," Dwayne said. "We're here to see the spokesman or public relations man or whatever you call him."

The young woman smiled and pushed a button. "Harry. Your visitors are here."

The man who came out gave them a polite smile. "I'm Harry Bailey. Come into my office." He led the way and gestured to two chairs as he sat down behind his desk. "Are you the private detective?"

"Yes, I am. This is Donna Sue Wheeler, my wife and secretary."

"Well then, what can I do for you?"

"Have you heard of a company called the *Hollywood Acting and Modeling Studio*?"

Bailey frowned. "Mmm, I can't say I have. Tell me something about it."

"It was a company that showed up in Wichita, Kansas, several months ago. They taught five girls about how to break into the movies. Then the organization took them in an airplane, supposedly to go to a studio here in Hollywood for screen tests and to become famous."

"Oh my god!" Harry Bailey stated as he leaned back in his chair and stared across the desk at Dwayne and Donna Sue. "I can assure you that they have not been here as far as I know. I'll look into it, but I'm confident that M-G-M had nothing to do with it. To be honest, it sounds to me like just another swindle."

"Okay," Dwayne said. "That's what we were afraid of. Thank you."

Bailey gave the two a close look. "Say! Would you two like to have a screen test? You really have a certain screen quality."

"No thanks," Dwayne said. "I'm a private eye, not an actor."

Donna Sue smiled. "But thank you."

———

THE NEXT STUDIO THE COUPLE VISITED WAS Paramount.

The head of public relations there was impressed. "So you're a real private detective, are you? I see a lot of private detectives around here, but they're all actors and not the real things."

"I can imagine that," Dwayne said. "Have you heard of the *Hollywood Acting and Modeling Studio*?"

"Nope."

"It's a phony outfit that came to Wichita, Kansas," Dwayne said.

Donna Sue explained, "They carried on with a sham school of telling young girls and their mothers they could be trained to go to Hollywood and get into the movies."

"I absolutely hate that!" the man uttered. "There are so many fraudulent people hanging around all the studios that it makes me sick. There was this photographer who would find pretty girls and tell them he could get them in the movies with his photographs. He would take the poor things out into the desert and strangle them. He killed seven before he was apprehended."

"How awful!" Donna Sue said with a shudder.

"Yeah," the man said. "Well...say! You two should take screen tests here at the Paramount studio. You both resemble the real thing when it comes to *noir* movies."

Dwayne was confused. "What's a *noir* movie?"

"They're films about cops, gangsters, and sexy women."

"No thanks." Dwayne grinned. "I get enough of that in real life without having to pretend!"

Donna Sue socked him lightly on the arm.

———

"OKAY, DWAYNE," DONNA SAID, LOOKING AT THE map. "Our next call will be Warner Brothers."

Half an hour later, they were seated before that studio's spokesman. "So you two are from Wichita, Kansas, huh? We've made a few westerns about Wichita."

"Well, we're an aircraft city now," Dwayne said, irritated a bit. He lit a Lucky Strike cigarette. "Are you acquainted with the *Hollywood Acting and Modeling Studio*?"

"Say what?"

"The *Hollywood Acting and Modeling Studio*," Donna Sue said. "They've kidnapped five girls under the pretense they are going to be made into movie actresses."

"Is that in Wichita?"

"Right," Dwayne said.

"Well, I've not come across that outfit," the spokesman told him. "That's too bad. Terrible, really. I hate things like that." He picked up a cigar from a box. "Would you like a cigar, Detective?"

"No, thanks."

The man lit the stogie and gazed at the couple. "You know something? You two ought to get a screen test."

"We're too busy," Dwayne replied.

———

"WELL, DWAYNE, LET'S HIT TWENTIETH Century."

"Okay. Give me the directions."

Once more, they went through an elaborate gate and were directed to the studio spokesman. The man asked them to sit down. "What can I do for you?"

Dwayne let Donna Sue speak for this one. "We have a possibly horrible happening in Wichita, Kansas. We think five schoolgirls have been kidnapped by a business called *Hollywood Acting and Modeling Studio*. We have visited Metro-Goldwyn-Mayer, Paramount, and Warner Brothers. Spokesmen for all three have stated that they know nothing about it and that the studios don't have anything to do with such operations."

The man leaned back in his chair. "So it seems the people in Wichita, Kansas, want to know the whereabouts of those youngsters. I don't blame them. I have a hobby of keeping track of dangerous people who prey on the ignorant when it comes to the movies. I don't mean the ignorant are stupid, they are just the victims of con artists." He pressed a buzzer summoning his secretary. "Julie, will you bring the files on the victimized persons."

The lady came in and handed off a thick cardboard jacket.

"Thank you," the man said. "Now. What was that name again?"

Dwayne said, "*Hollywood Acting and Modeling Studio.*"

"Right." The man reached into the jacket and pulled out a folder. He went through the contents but after several minutes, shook his head. "Sorry. I don't have it."

Dwayne and Donna Sue looked at each other with expressions of regret. For a moment, they had hoped that this visit would provide an actual clue.

"That's too bad," the spokesman said sympathetically. He studied the couple. "Would you two be interested in a screen test?"

"No, but thanks," Donna Sue said, not surprised at the suggestion by this point.

"Since when did we become William Powell and Myrna Loy?" Dwayne asked as they went out to their car.

Donna Sue studied him. "I don't know. I think you

look more like Gary Cooper. And I bear a certain resemblance to Jean Arthur."

Dwayne laughed. "Jean Harlow is more like it. And I'm a dead ringer for Clark Gable without the mustache."

Donna Sue chuckled and took his arm. "Come on, Clark."

———

DWAYNE AND DONNA SUE WENT BACK TO THE hotel and showered then took naps after the tour. In the early evening, they went to the café next to the hotel. The waitress stood waiting to take their order.

"I see the evening fare is Mexican," Dwayne remarked.

"Yes, sir," the waitress said.

"We're from Wichita, Kansas. We got a Mexican restaurant called the *El Charro Café.*"

"You just said two articles, sir. 'El' and 'the' meant the same thing."

Dwayne opened his eyes wide. "I never knew that!"

"Are you ready to order, sir?"

"I think I'll have the taco dinner."

"It's enchiladas for me," Donna Sue said.

After being served, they ate slowly, savoring a different taste from Wichita's Mexican eatery. For dessert, they ate *helado chocolate,* i.e., chocolate ice cream.

They went back to the hotel. "What do you think of those offers of screen tests?" Dwayne asked.

"I'm not for it," Donna Sue said. "I don't want you kissing Betty Grable."

"Oh, yeah? Well, I don't want Cary Grant kissing you. So there!"

Chapter 23

It was one more breakfast in the café, then Dwayne and Donna Sue went to the hotel parking lot and got into their rented Ford.

"What does that map say?" Dwayne asked.

"Fox."

"I don't want to know about any animals," Dwayne said irritably.

"It's not an animal, Dwayne. It's Fox Studio."

"Oh! Give me the directions."

When they reached the studio, the couple went through the gate and followed the guard's directions to an office building. The head of public relations at Fox was a short man with a wig that was easy to see.

"So you're the detective we've heard about?"

"Yeah," Dwayne said. "This is my wife and secretary."

"Okay. What do you want?"

"Well, we're from Wichita, Kansas," Dwayne began. "And an outfit called the *Hollywood Acting and Modeling Studio* showed up saying they wanted to get some girls."

"What kind of girls?"

"The kind of ones that just graduated from high school."

"Okay, got it."

Donna Sue cleared her throat. "There were five and the last anyone saw of them was when they were flying away from the Wichita Airport."

"Gotcha," the spokesman said. "And the people that took 'em was called what again?"

"*Hollywood Acting and Modeling Studio*," Dwayne told him.

"Right!" The man picked up his phone. "Erika, darling, connect me to the Bureau of Cinema Enterprises, please." He hung up. "Sometimes the people in the movie world are hard to get to."

His phone rang again, and he answered it. "Hello. This is the Bureau of Cinema Enterprises, right? Charley Peters at Fox. What do you have on an organization by the name of *Hollywood Acting and Modeling Studio*? Not in Hollywood. What about Los Angeles? San Diego? San Francisco? Okay, thank you." He looked at Dwayne and Donna Sue. "Well, there's no company you're talking about anywhere in California."

Dwayne and Donna Sue stood up. "Well, thank you for your time."

The man gave the couple an inviting look. "Say! Would you—"

"No, thank you," Dwayne said, holding up a hand to interrupt the question. "We don't want a screen test."

"Well, if you're sure. Here, take my card in case you change your mind."

———

"WHO'S NEXT?" DWAYNE ASKED.

"RKO Productions."

"Give me the directions."

"As you wish, my love," Donna Sue remarked. "I'll be kind to you since RKO is close by."

They went through the entrance routine and found themselves sitting in front of yet another spokesman. He was a gruff old man who seemed impatient. He was mostly bald and had a brush of a mustache.

"What's your problem, Detective?" he asked.

Dwayne took a deep breath. "We're from Wichita, Kansas, and are tracking down some young ladies who were kidnapped."

"Wichita, huh? Ya know, I'm from Oklahoma. Hobart, Oklahoma, that is. I have a grandson who works at Cessna Aircraft in Wichita." The man paused. He didn't seem as impatient as he went on. "Now tell me about these young ladies getting kidnapped."

Dwayne went through his *Hollywood Acting and Modeling Studio* routine.

"Ya know, Dwayne—you too, Donna Sue—I've been in this business since I come out here in nineteen and twenty-one to seek my fortune in California. I didn't do too good 'til a feller I ran into told me in a bar that I had that cowboy look. So I started working in cowboy films and then I wrote up a few Western film stories and then I got to directing 'em. Well, wouldn't you know it, but this ol' Okie from Hobart got a production office all of my own for a while. Now I'm stuck here in this office being a spokesman for the studio while younger fellas get to make the pictures."

"That's interesting," Dwayne said.

"Yes it is," Donna Sue said.

"Well, I don't know nothing about no model studio in Wichita. But listen up. Dwayne, you're a tough looker and Donna Sue, you're just as cute as can be. You two should do a screen test." The man pointed across the desk. "You know, with a couple like you lined up for a picture, they might let me direct again."

"We want to rescue those girls before we do anything about screen tests," Dwayne said.

"Well, you two, you know where I am if'n you wanna be in the movies." The man got a faraway look in his eyes. "We could call it *The Cowboy and the Saloon Girl...*"

"WHERE ARE WE GOING NEXT?" DWAYNE ASKED.

"Columbia Pictures. It isn't real close."

Twenty-five minutes later, Dwayne pulled into the entrance of Columbia. The guard looked at their identification, then told them how to get to the main office where the public relations department was located.

When Dwayne and Donna Sue walked into the office, the man stood up behind his desk and offered a hand. "Glad to see you two. I see that you are a detective and secretary from Wichita, Kansas. Do you have any *noir* scripts to sell? It's a very popular type of movie right now."

"We learned what *noir* is when we arrived here yesterday," Donna Sue said. "But my husband has an actual crime to solve. It is about the kidnapping of five young women."

The man sat down. "I see. This is a real crime, not a script, right?"

"That's what she said," Dwayne remarked, a little irritated. This was serious business, not Hollywood make-believe. He began explaining about the *Hollywood Acting and Modeling Studio* along with the girls and their disappearance.

"That is terrible!" the man said. "I've been around movies for a long time and have seen a lot of mean people pulling criminal tricks and taking money from girls and women who want to be stars. But I have never heard of your exact problem. Sorry."

"Well, thanks for your time."

He watched them start for the door. "Would you two like to take--?"

"No thanks," Dwayne said before the man could finish getting the question out.

———

"THIS IS NEXT TO THE LAST," DONNA SAID. "IT'S Universal Studio."

Once again, Dwayne and Donna found themselves in front of a spokesman's desk. And once again, the man had never heard of *Hollywood Acting and Modeling Studio*, and they didn't want to have a screen test.

Dwayne drove out of the gate and saw something he thought amusing. It was a restaurant in the shape of a weenie. It had a sign advertising hot dogs. "Look at that!"

Donna Sue laughed. "Let's eat lunch there."

Dwayne pulled up into the parking lot. They went inside and ordered their food. Dwayne asked for two hot dogs, french fries, and Orange Crush. That was close to his favorite lunch, except he couldn't order a grilled cheese sandwich. Donna Sue was served a hot dog and Coke. They enjoyed their lunch and ate slowly.

When they left, Dwayne asked what the last studio would be.

"Let me look at the map," Donna Sue said. "Mmm, United Artists. Hey, this is interesting."

"What's interesting?"

"It says here that United Artists was founded by D.W. Griffith, Charlie Chaplin, Mary Pickford, and Douglas Fairbanks. I see why it is named United Artists. The artists who own it were united."

Dwayne chuckled, "*United* studio in the *United* States."

"Dwayne, I'm going to say something to you that Fibber McGee and Molly do on the radio. 'T'ain't funny, McGee."

"Well, lookie here," Dwayne said. "It's United Artists."

Once more, they went through being ushered to the office of a spokesman. And once more, the *Hollywood Acting and Modeling Studio* was unknown to him. And once again, there was an offering of screen tests, and once more, Dwayne and Donna Sue turned it down.

When they drove off the lot, Donna Sue asked, "Now what will we do?"

"I think we should go to the Los Angeles Police and call on their Missing Persons Bureau."

————

DWAYNE AND DONNA SUE WALKED INTO THE lobby of the Los Angeles Police Department. A sergeant looked up at them from his desk. "What can I do for you?"

Dwayne showed him his badge and permit. The sergeant looked at them. "Wichita, Kansas. You've come a long way. What's your request?"

"We would like to go to the Missing Persons Department. It involves five teenage girls who have either been kidnapped or have dropped out of sight. They were last seen flying from Wichita to Hollywood."

"Okay. Go up to the second floor and turn right to walk down the hall to the end."

"Thanks," Dwayne said.

The two followed the directions and went to the counter of the Missing Persons Bureau. A clerk walked up to them.

"Yeah?"

"We'd like to report the disappearance of five teenage girls who left on an airplane in Wichita for what was supposed to be a trip to Hollywood."

Donna Sue spoke up. "We have portrait photos of all of them."

The clerk nodded. "That's good. What are they to you?"

Once again, Dwayne spoke. "Here's my badge and permit from the State of Kansas. I'm hired to track down the lost girls."

"Okay, I've got your caper," the clerk said. "But let me tell you something. The girls who want to be actresses in the movies and go missing are found alive or dead. Mostly it's the latter. So I'd advise you not to get your hopes up." He pulled out some papers from under the counter. "Fill this out."

Donna Sue did the writing because of her good penmanship. When she finished, the clerk came over to get the photos and the papers. "We'll do our best."

"Thanks," Dwayne said.

He and Donna Sue walked back down the hall and to the entrance of the building. They reached the car and headed for the Hotel Floras Lindas.

"Well, sweetie," Dwayne said. "I dread having to tell

the families that we couldn't find a thing." He paused. "But we'll tell them that we turned their daughters' case over to the Missing Persons Bureau in the Los Angeles Police Department."

"We're never going to find those poor girls, are we?"

Dwayne didn't say anything. Right now, he couldn't think of a single thing more that they could do.

CHAPTER 24

Madam Ekaterina Lobanovska was born into the high society of Imperial Russia. However, when she was in her teens, the Communists took over their country in the Russian Revolution and ruined the good life of the affluent class.

Her uncle, Boris Lobanovski, was the Russian ambassador to the Republic of Mexico. When he learned his family was in a dangerous predicament, he quickly acted. The first thing he did was to make it possible for his family in Russia to send their money and valuables over to *el Banco de México,* i.e., the Bank of Mexico. He was a very intelligent man and he quickly exchanged the Russian rubles for Mexican pesos.

Then he arranged for them to get out of what was once Imperial Russia and flee to Paris, France. From Paris, they traveled to the port of Marseille and embarked to Mexico to be reunited with Boris.

The family—father Dmitri Lobanovski; mother Doroteya Lobanovska; two brothers, Aleksandr and Vladimir Lobanovski; and three sisters, Ekaterina, Anastasia, and Anna Lobanovska—arrived at the port of Veracruz after crossing the Atlantic Ocean. Uncle Boris was there to meet them. He had hired a bus to take them to a mountain hacienda—which was referred to as the name *H*acienda with a capital *H*—above the ocean town of Marpoco.

The Lobanovski family was surprised by the location. There was Uncle Boris's country dwelling along with the *péones*, i.e. peasants who were like the *skrepostnoi* i.e., serfs of Russia. Those hardworking Mexicans lived in adobe huts in the hills around the Hacienda. They planted corn, beans, peppers and butchered pigs, goats, and chickens.

When the *péones* took their crops and meats down to Marpoco, they put it all on their burros' strong little backs. After the sales, they kept a quarter of the harvest and turned three-quarters over to Boris Lobanovski. A team of *gerentes*, i.e., bosses, made sure the division was accurate.

———

THE MEXICAN TOWN OF MARPOCO WAS LOCATED on the northeastern coast of the country. The population was five thousand people, and it had a small harbor where freighters docked. Those ships weren't exactly sleek in appearance because of the rust that ran down their hulls, but they were still seaworthy.

Marpoco also had an airport that dealt with passengers and cargo. They had one airplane, a Ford Trimotor. It was built by the Stout Metal Airplane Division of the Ford Motor Company. It flew up to Nogales, Texas, USA, and back to Marpoco's airport.

A detachment of *Infanteria de Marina*, i.e., Marine Infantry, was stationed on the docks. This military group patrolled the coastal area and inspected the cargo dropped off by the freighters. They earned quite a few pesos through bribes.

The three neighborhoods of Marpoco were, first, that of the upper class that looked down on the other inhabitants. These were few, but powerful in that they were the wealthy politicians, wealthy businessmen, and a very wealthy banker.

The second was the middle class who were the grocery owners, restaurateurs, merchandisers, carpenters, bartenders, etc. Down at the bottom of this group were the shoe shiners, janitors, streetsweepers, and others.

There was the final step down and that involved sex. Three bordellos catered to the rich and middle class. The worn-out old prostitutes had shacks on the docks.

————

THE LIFE OF THE LOBANOVSKI CLAN IN Hacienda was pleasant and enjoyable. There were servants, cooks, and gardeners serving them. The father Dmitri Lobanovski didn't take it easy. He worked for his older brother who had rescued him and his wife and children from the Communists.

Therefore, he labored hard to keep the bills balanced correctly, managing the *gerentes*, and keeping a sharp inspection on all parts of Hacienda.

Every few weeks Dmitri Lobanovski rode one of the horses through the adobe cabins of the *péones* to see how they were getting along. This wasn't out of kindness, it was because of the possibility of problems. However, the *péone* families were kind to each other. Their sick and injured were treated by a very old sorceress, a *bruja*. And if any person had problems, the rest of the village was more than happy to help them.

Mother Doroteya Lobanovska taught her daughters the same as she did in Russia. There was knitting, painting, crocheting, and playing the piano. Three maids of the *péone* village had been carefully chosen to serve the young ladies.

The Lobanovski young men Aleksandr and Vladimir were happier in Mexico than they had been in Imperial Russia. In the military, the lads had been forced into commissions of junior lieutenants in the Imperial Army Cavalry. They didn't mind the Army horses, but the discipline was horrendous.

Aleksandr and Vladimir were happy to discover that there was a stable in Hacienda with two stallions. The noble horses were taken care of by the *Jefe de Caballos,* i.e., the Chief of Horses. He was impressed when he saw the skill of the two young men in the saddle.

Uncle Boris kept a Duisenberg 12-cylinder sedan in the garage. It was driven by Pedro, the chauffeur, and he was worried every time he saw Aleksandr and Vladimir drive it out of Hacienda and down to the town of Marpoco.

They always parked in front of the same bordello. The prostitutes thought the two Russians were cute from the way they spoke Spanish. During the evenings, the lads went up the stairs two or three times to have sex with the women. When Aleksandr and Vladimir were tired and drunk, they got in the automobile and drove back up the mountain to Hacienda.

As visits became more often, the girls began to like them. Even *Doña* Rosa Gomez, who was the brothel's matron, found the brothers likable. Many times she invited the brothers upstairs to her apartment where they joked and drank madeira wine. The two Russian youths never made advances at her. Such things were just not done.

———

Ten years passed and the Lobanovski family was happy and satisfied in their life. However, there were no young men in the area suitable to marry their daughters. When Uncle Boris began to help Imperial Russian families escape from the Communists, the problem of finding young men for the daughters evaporated. Their families all lived in *Ciudad de México* i.e., Mexico City and their new wives joined them there.

However, Ekatrina was not interested in marriage. She loved the Hacienda and didn't want to leave. Her father Dmitri did not want to force his oldest daughter into matrimony if she was disinterested, so Ekaterina remained there with her parents and brothers.

———

One day in 1935, a caller appeared at the door of the Hacienda. He was Victor Delgado, an *abogado,* i.e., lawyer. He was escorted to Dmitri's office and informed the Russian that he had news for his two sons.

When Aleksandr and Vladimir showed up, Delgado showed them a legal document. "*Caballeros, Doña* Rosa Gomez has died and left all of her bordello to you."

Dmitri was not pleased. "I do not want my sons to become pimps."

Delgado shrugged. "I have served *Doña* Rosa and her bordello for twenty years. Its value is two hundred thousand pesos. That's fifty thousand dollars American."

The Hacienda had grown more and more expensive to operate, and Dmitri became thoughtful for a minute or so.

The *abodado* waited patiently.

Dmitri turned to his sons. "Sign the paper."

———

MORE YEARS PASSED AND DMITRI LOBANVOSKI died. The Hacienda was harder to manage than ever. The *péones* were beginning to leave to go down to live on the outskirts of Marpoco. There was more work and more money to be earned in jobs that were half as hard as farming.

Ekatrina and her brothers ended up depending on the bordello for their livelihood. Then a tragedy occurred one night when Aleksandr and Vladimir were going up the road to Hacienda and were extremely intoxicated. Vladimir, who was driving, missed a turn and went over a cliff. Both were killed instantly in the flaming crash.

Now Ekatrina had to deal with the bordello on her own. She did well keeping it open, knowing Hacienda was safe. On one visit to the brothel to get the weekly earnings, she met a new prostitute who had showed up. The woman Marlya was in her thirties and had been selling sex since she was fourteen years old. In one of their conversations, Marlya told Ekatrina about how Arabian men were fond of white women, especially if they were virgins.

Ekatrina, now calling herself Madam Lobanovska, had an idea.

CHAPTER 25

Dwayne and Donna Sue had gone over to the McNally house to report on their California trip. The rest of the families came to join them there. They already knew about Dwayne and Donna Sue's failure to find their daughters, but they wanted to hear what went on during their visit to California.

Margret McNally had made coffee, but Carolyn Taylor said, "I don't feel like this is a party."

Margret's Irish temper blazed. "I did not say this was a *party, Carolyn!*"

Stanley Watson spoke, "Let's not get angry, okay? Things are bad enough." He turned to Dwayne. "So what happened?"

"Okay. We went to eight studios. In each we met with a representative of the studio. They were kind and sympathetic about your daughter's disappearance. It seems that many young women try to get into the movies and wind up badly. But none of the spokesmen knew anything about the *Hollywood Acting and Modeling Studio.*"

"Oh god!" Rachel Carlson said.

Donna Sue said, "We went to the Los Angeles Police Department's Missing Person's Bureau."

"Yeah," Dwayne said. "We left pictures of each girl and gave them my phone number to call if they find out anything."

"Thank you, Dwayne and Donna Sue, for your efforts," Oskar Hanson said. He sighed. "It seems we were all doomed to failure from the beginning."

CHAPTER 26

It was a half hour after the evening dinner when the five girls were seated around the table that had been cleared off by Ahab, the chef's Mexican boy.

Claudine Ginnette sensed something in the air. The girls uttered no sounds; they were untalkative and somber. Several times they glared hatefully at her. Kari Hanson was as quiet as her companions.

Then suddenly she stood up and made a declaration. "I am a Lutheran. Yes! I am a Lutheran!"

Molly McNally looked over at Kari and joined her. "I am a Catholic!"

"I am a Presbyterian!" Jennie Watson announced as she stood up. "Yes!"

"And I am a Methodist," Rachel Carlson joined them.

Carolyn Taylor didn't hesitate as she got to her feet. "I am a Baptist!"

Claudine Ginnette wondered what the girls were doing and was suddenly very nervous. Kari turned to face the French woman.

"You!" she shrieked. "All of your Cauls are from hell. And that's where you're going to go."

"You are right!" Jennie said. She pointed a finger at Claudine. "And your enlightenment is false!"

Claudine was wary as she stood up. "What do you mean?"

"The Exotic Dance is the gyration of the Devil," Carolyn Taylor shouted.

All five were standing up and glaring at the frightened Claudine.

Kari: "Our Father which art in heaven, hallowed be thy name..."

Jennie: "Thy kingdom come, thy will be done on earth as it is in heaven..."

Molly: "Give us this day our daily bread..."

Rachel: "And forgive us our debts, as we forgive our debtors..."

Carolyn: "And lead us not into temptation, but deliver us from evil..."

All: "For this is the kingdom and the power and the glory forever...Amen!"

Kari pointed at Claudine. "Did you hear what we said? I will repeat it; deliver us from evil!"

The girls walked menacingly toward Claudine. There was no doubt they wanted to get their hands around the French woman's neck. They had finally figured out that they outnumbered her five to one, and no matter what else happened to them, they could at least get their revenge on her for leading them into this nightmare.

Claudine suddenly ran to her bed and grabbed her suitcase. The terrified woman headed in panic for the door. Kari lunged at her, trying to intercept her, but Claudine darted nimbly around the girl. She unlocked the door and went outside, stopping to relock the portal just in time as the girls hammered furiously with their fists on the other side. Then she continued running toward the mansion.

When the French woman reached it, she shouted out. "Help me!"

Emeryk, the Polish bodyguard, opened the door. "What is it you want?"

"I must speak with Madam Lobanovska. Please!"

She was led into the interior of the mansion to Madam Lobanovska's living room. The Russian woman was surprised. "What is it, Claudine? You should be with your charges."

"I think the girls are going crazy!"

Madam Lobanovska smiled. "I think you are tired. You want maybe to go see your lover. Is not that what you want?"

"Oh, yes!"

"Of course. You must do that." She turned to Emeryk. "Get car and drive Miss Claudine down to Marpoco."

———

CLAUDINE GINNETTE GOT OUT OF THE CAR WHEN it pulled up in front of her house in Marpoco's better neighborhood. She went to the door and used a key to get into the house. No lights were on and she tiptoed to the bedroom she used with Jacques. After turning on the lamp, she looked around and saw the bed was empty.

She decided to get a negligee from the closet. She slid the door open and reached in, then noticed that all of Jacques's clothing was gone. Gwendoline's bedroom was upstairs, so she decided to go up and see about Jacques's absence.

When Claudine reached the door, she walked in, then

stopped. The moonlight was shining on the bed, and she saw that Gwendoline was sleeping with Jacques. Claudine let out a startled, angry exclamation.

Both Gwendoline and Jacques bolted awake and sat up to look over at her. Gwendolyn clutched the sheet to her breasts. The Frenchman sighed. "Well, Claudine. Gwendoline and I have fallen in love. That is all there is to it, and you must accept it."

Claudine stood openmouthed, then turned slowly and went downstairs to her bedroom. When her anger over what she had seen finally ebbed, she grew cold. Claudine wanted revenge, but not on the girls. She desired to get even with Gwendolyn and Jacques, but especially Gwendolyn.

She picked up her suitcase and walked the short way to the town plaza in Marpoco. She caught a cab and went out to the Marpoco *Aeropuerto,* i.e., airport. She entered the terminal building and headed for the ticket counter.

She walked up and told the agent, "*Quiero un billete, por favor.*"

"*Si, señorita. Dónde quiere ir?*" the agent asked.

"*A Los Estados Unidos,*" Claudine said.

"*En cual ciudad, señorita?*" the agent asked.

"Wichita, Kansas," Claudine said.

CHAPTER 27

Dwayne Wheeler returned to the office from his latest caper. He had been hired as a guard while the New York City Art Museum unloaded their paintings to be displayed in the Forum. This was a traveling show that was going around to several cities in the Midwest.

Donna Sue looked up as he walked through the door. "How'd it go?"

"Well," he said. "They kept the exhibits covered, so I didn't see one piece of art. However, I was paid fifty bucks cash. Not bad for five hours of standing around." He hung his fedora on the hat rack. "Any calls for further capers?"

"Nope."

Dwayne sat down at his desk. He just started to make the notes of the art museum caper when Donna Sue let out a yell. He immediately walked back to the front office. "What's going on?"

Donna Sue pointed at the door. "Look who's here."

Dwayne's eyes opened wide. "Well, well. Here's a French lady that's showed up."

Claudine Ginnette, fatigued from the flight from Marpoco, Mexico, stated, "I know where the five girls are."

Donna Sue was concerned. She stood up and asked, "Are they okay?"

"They are well-fed and safe. But I do not know how long that will be true."

"Where are they?" Dwayne asked.

"In a hacienda on a mountain above the seaside village of Marpoco in northeastern Mexico."

"In Mexico!" Dwayne shouted.

"You had better move fast if you want to rescue them. They are trapped in white slavery and will be auctioned off to wealthy Arab oil magnates."

"Goddammit!" Dwayne cursed. He was glad to know that the girls were alive, but from the sound of it, they were in great danger.

Donna Sue looked at Dwayne. "We better get upstairs to see Terry McCarthy."

"Let's go." He took Claudine Ginnette's arm and followed Donna Sue up to the third floor, where the Wichita office of the Federal Bureau of Investigation was located. Dwayne had worked with both the FBI and the Kansas Bureau of Investigation in the past, although not always completely willingly. In some cases, he had pitched in to help the G-Men when his own shady activities threatened to get him into deeper trouble.

The three arrived at the office and the secretary looked up, alarmed by the sudden intrusion. "What in the world is—"

The trio ignored her and went through the door and startled Terry McCarthy, the agent in charge of the local office. McCarthy put his hands on his desk, pushed to his feet, and asked, "What's going on, Dwayne? I know you wouldn't come busting in this way if it wasn't something important."

"This little gal knows exactly where those five girls are. They're on the northeast coast of Mexico, up in the mountains."

"Five girls—" McCarthy's eyes widened. Dwayne had told him about the caper and the unsuccessful visit to Hollywood. "You mean the ones who fell for that movie swindle and disappeared?"

"That's right." Dwayne nodded at Claudine. "This lady was part of it, but now she wants to help the girls."

He had no idea why Claudine had decided to double-cross her partners in the scheme, but he wasn't going to worry about that now. That could be hashed out later, once the girls were safe.

Claudine had to have a pretty powerful motive, though, since she was putting her own neck on the line.

McCarthy went to the door leading to his secretary's office. "Get Jim Ferguson! Now!" He went back, looking at Claudine Ginnette. "Are the girls okay?"

"Yes. There is a lady who wants to sell them to rich Arabian oilmen. The girls are blonds, redheads...and virgins."

"Yeah," McCarthy said. "That's their taste in women. Who is this lady boss?"

Claudine continued. "She is a Russian and wants to sell them for a half-million dollars."

The secretary spoke up. "Agent Ferguson is on the phone."

McCarthy picked up his phone. "Hello, Jim. Remember those five missing girls Dwayne Wheeler told me about? We now have what we need to rescue them. It seems they're down in Mexico, being held by white slavers, and might be sold to Arabs." He listened to his boss and picked up a pencil and pad. "Yeah. I can start taking notes."

The FBI man scribbled on the pad and turned a lot of pages. Finally, after twenty minutes, he hung up.

"Okay, Listen, Dwayne. I wrote all this down. Jim said he'll be flying from Washington to McConnell Air Force Base. He's bringing two more agents with him. I'll be going too. And he wants you."

"Me?" Dwayne said.

"Yeah. And he wants Donna Sue to come along too. She can take care of the five girls once we've rescued them. He also wants a member of the Wichita Police Department to go along as a representative because the girls are Wichitans."

"I know just the guy," Dwayne said. "Sergeant Al Gallagher, a homicide detective. I used to couldn't stand the guy, but he kind of grew on me when we worked on a caper together a while back."

"Great!" McCarthy continued. "Be sure and bring along this woman who reported where the girls are. There is an FBI liaison in that part of Mexico, a *Federale* named Juan DeLario. We'll fly from McConnell Air Force Base to the airport in the town of Marpoco. The Mexican Marines will be waiting for us there to drive up the mountain road. And, number one importance, do not, I say again, do not inform the girls' families until we get back. We may have missed them. In that case, the FBI will inform them."

"Damn those white slavers!" Dwayne said through gritted teeth. He had been mixed up in some crooked rackets in the past, but nothing to compare with this. Rage at what had been done to those girls burned inside him.

CHAPTER 28

Dwayne and Donna Sue rushed home to get ready for the mission. He hurriedly went to one of the doorjambs and carefully removed the slat. He pulled out three Tommy guns and ammunition drums that held a hundred rounds each.

Donna Sue was alarmed. "What are you going to do with those?"

"I'm gonna take them with us for the raid. I'll take one, give one to Al Gallagher and one to Terry McCarthy." He reached back into the doorjamb and pulled out three boxes of .45 caliber ammunition. Then he carefully put the slat back in its place.

With that done, Dwayne put on green overalls and a web harness that held his automatic .45 pistol along with holders for six ammo magazines. He looked over at his wife.

"I'm ready to go kick ass, honey."

"You be careful, Dwayne!"

Donna Sue dressed in a jacket, blouse, slacks, and flat leather shoes. She took a large purse to wear over her shoulder. She also put on one of Dwayne's baseball hats to round out her outfit.

————

A C-47 LANDED AT McCONNELL AIR BASE IN THE early evening on that same day.

The group waiting for it consisted of Dwayne, Donna Sue, Terry McCarthy, Sergeant Al Gallagher, and Claudine Ginnette. Claudine was a prisoner but was not hand-cuffed or restrained in any other way. So far, she had shown no signs of backing out.

She wanted to be in at the kill.

Dwayne had given McCarthy and Al each a Tommy gun while keeping one for himself. That was a lot of fire-power, but they might need it before this caper was over.

The new arrivals were Chief FBI Agent Jim Fergus-son, Larry Duncan, and Daniel Greenbern. Fergusson called everyone together and addressed them while the airplane was being gassed up for the flight to Mexico.

"Now listen up," Fergusson said. "We're not going to have much conversation on the noisy flight down there. I can't give you much information about our tactics, but we will meet up with Commander Francisco Catalon of the Mexican Marines that are stationed in the small city of Marpoco. It's on a harbor, but we don't need to be worried about that since we'll be moving up an inland mountain road." He paused. "I want you men to be ready to go into combat." He smiled and nodded to Donna Sue and Claudine. "I see our ladies will be ready to take care of the five girls after they are rescued."

Terry McCarthy raised his hand. "What about those Marines? Will they lead us or do they follow?"

"They *follow us*, of course, Terry. Our agent, Juan DeLario, will have things set up for the assault."

———

THE SEATING ON THE C-47 RAN DOWN BOTH sides of the fuselage. The group gazed across at each other, solemn as they set out on this mission because the fates of five innocent girls were riding on them. The loud droning of the airplane's engines began to have an effect, though. Several of them nodded off, dozing, and a couple sank into a deep sleep.

The flight continued soaring down across Oklahoma and Texas and over Mexico on the way to the mission.

The eventual change in the engines' roar brought the outfit awake. As eyes opened, the adrenaline began to rise. The thought of a battle was foremost on their minds.

The landing at the Marpoco Airport was smooth, and a signalman on the runway waved the flashlights in his hands over to where the C-47 was to park. Everyone got off the airplane and immediately saw Mexican federal policeman and FBI liaison Juan DeLario who had an office in Mexico City.

"Hello, Juan," Jim Ferguson said.

DeLario gave him a serious look. "Be ready to get pissed off."

"Shit! Are those girls gone now?"

DeLario shook his head. "Oh, no. They are still up there in that hacienda." He pointed. "Here comes your problem now."

An officer of the *Infanteria de Marina*, i.e., Marine Infantry, walked up. He stopped and looked at the six men and two women.

"Welcome to Marpoco, Mexico." He spoke in perfect

English. "My rank and name is Commander Francisco Catalon of the Mexican Marines." He showed a big grin and looked over at Agent Juan DeLario. "Hello, Juan. Which of you is in charge?"

Juan pointed to Ferguson. Jim Ferguson stepped forward. "That would be me, Commander Catalon. I am Chief FBI Agent James Ferguson."

"I see. You look like you are going to a war, eh?"

"A small raid, Commander."

The Marine officer pointed to where a jeep and a truck were parked. "I will be going up the mountain road to the hacienda with those two vehicles."

Ferguson growled. "We are here to rescue five American girls."

"I am aware of that, Chief Agent Ferguson. But this is Mexico, and I am standing on Mexican soil and will do things my way." He looked again at the Americans. "And you won't be needing those three Tommy guns and all the other firearms you have brought."

Ferguson knew he had to obey him.

Commander Francisco Catalon pointed to the jeep and truck. "I want you, Ferguson, and DeLario, as well as those two women, to walk over and get into the vehicles with me."

As the group walked off, Sergeant Al Gallagher looked over at Dwayne and said, "What the hell are we supposed to do, shamus?"

"Damned if I know," Dwayne said. "I don't like this any more than you go, Gallagher." He sighed. "But I don't suppose we can fight the Mexican Marines."

———

THE VEHICLES WENT RAPIDLY UP THE MOUNTAIN road to the hacienda and turned onto the path to the entrance door. A man with a pistol holster on his belt looked at the group. He started to draw his weapon.

Commander Catalon got his out quicker and snarled, "You will open the door or I will shoot you. And come over here and hand my driver your *pistola*."

The man, frightened by the Marine officer, obeyed.

The two vehicles went through the opening and headed straight for the mansion. They pulled up at the portal, and Commander Francisco Catalon, Chief Agent Jim Ferguson, Agent Juan DeLario, Donna Sue Wheeler, and Claudine Ginnette got out of the Jeep while the two Marine drivers stayed where they were.

The Polish servant Emeryk was standing on the mansion porch. He looked at the arrivals. The Commander said, "We are here to speak to Madam Lobanova."

Emeryk turned around and opened the door. "Follow with me."

The five people who had entered were ushered by Emeryk into an office. Madam Ekatrina Lobanovska was surprised to see them. She spoke in fluent Spanish. "What is it you want, *Comandante*?"

"Madam Lobanovska, I have been informed of the five American girls being held prisoner here."

The Russian woman was surprised. "Who told you that, *Comandante*?"

"Do not play me for a fool!" the *Comandante* declared. "I have come to rescue them."

Madam Lobanovska stuttered. "Why...they have... they have not been harmed. They are guests here."

"You have some very evil plans for them. Were you going to sell them?"

The Russian woman began breathing hard.

"Are you a white slaver, madam? Yes! That's what you are, and I am going to order you to send five thousand dollars to each of the young women's families. Where are they, Madam Lobanovska?"

"They are in their bungalow," she said and turned to Emeryk. "Take them to the *Americanas*."

Emeryk nodded and led them out of the mansion across Hacienda. He knocked on the door and Gwendolyn Haversham answered.

Emeryk said, "Here the Americans to take away girls." He abruptly left.

Gwendolyn had a pistol in a holster. Commander Catalon reached over and took the weapon. She swallowed hard, then called out to the girls in a shaky voice. "They are here for you."

The five girls were stunned, but they rushed out, talking rapidly and trembling with relief at their rescue

Kari Hanson said to Donna Sue, "You are the lady across the hall from the studio, aren't you."

"Yes," Donna Sue replied. "Now let's get you back to wonderful Wichita, Kansas."

Claudine Ginnette frowned at Gwendolyn and looked like she wanted to claw the English woman's eyes out.

"Do not be mad at me, Claudine. I know you betrayed us because of your anger over me and Jacques, but he...he is dead. His plane crashed."

"Really?" Claudine said. "Well, you must excuse me now. I must go with these people to sign my papers that will make me an American citizen."

That wasn't the deal she had made with the American authorities at all, but she was glad to let Gwendolyn think that.

Molly McNally came up, and with no warning, hit Gwendolyn with a hard slap across her face. "Go get our suitcases."

Jennie Watson, Rachel Carlson, and Carolyn Taylor began pulling her hair, slapping her face and kicking her buttocks as she stumbled to get the luggage. Catalon called out to his men to restrain the girls before they got too carried away.

They wanted to go after Claudine, too, but Jim Ferguson told them, "She saved you, girls. Without her, no one would have known where you were."

Donna Sue felt sorry for Claudine, despite the horrible thing the French woman had done, and finally led her outside the gate.

"I'll be going to jail when we get back to Kansas, won't I?" Claudine asked.

"Probably," Donna Sue said. "But the fact that you helped rescue those girls will probably cause the judge to be lenient on you, at least to a certain extent."

"I don't care," Claudine said. "As long as that bitch Gwendolyn is locked up, too!"

THE GIRLS WERE TRUCKED DOWN TO MARPOCO'S airport. Commander Catalon shook hands with the FBI agents as well as Dwayne and Al Gallagher.

"It all has turned out fine," the Marine Commander said. "When those devil Russians moved into this area, they brought with them an evil way of life."

"What will happen to that Russian lady?" Donna Sue asked.

Catalon shrugged. "She will sit up there in that cursed

Hacienda and harass her *péones*. There is only so much we can do."

"Are you going to make sure she sends that five thousand American dollars to the girls' parents?"

"I will keep that promise. I can bring that much pressure on her."

As the Americans got into the C-47, Chief FBI Jim Ferguson called Dwayne Wheeler, FBI Agent Terry McCarthy and Sergeant Al Gallagher. They were carrying the Tommy guns.

Ferguson spoke to Dwayne. "I think you owe the United States government something."

Dwayne frowned. "What do I owe the United States government?"

"Those three Tommy guns," Ferguson growled. "They are the ones that were stolen from that ambush when you were hauling illegal cigarettes."

"Oh!" Dwayne said as if surprised. "*Those* Tommy guns!"

————

CHIEF FBI JAMES FERGUSON HAD ARRANGED FOR a press conference in the Wichita City Hall. The newspapers *Wichita Eagle* and *Wichita Beason* along with radio stations KFH and KANS were invited.

Ferguson started his remarks with, "I am going to make a brief statement. I will not answer questions." He paused. "Five Wichita girls were kidnapped and taken out of the United States. Those five girls are now back in Wichita unharmed. Thank you."

He walked out with the press, yelling at him for more information but never looked back.

CHAPTER 29

Dwayne and Donna Sue Wheeler settled down to a satisfying set of capers. There was that New York City Art Museum exhibit continuing; an escort of Pete Driscoll the fence to find a stolen diamond ring; catching a thief who had been prowling the Royal Arms Apartments; two bond problems with A.J. Kessler; and last but not least, finding the stolen car of a traveling salesman who was stranded in Wichita.

Donna Sue found out that twenty-five thousand American dollars had been sent to be divided up between the Hanson, Watson, McNally, Carlson, and Taylor families. Commander Francisco Catalon had kept his word about getting Madam Ekatrina Lobanovska to send the money.

It wasn't justice for what had been done, but it was something.

The rescue of the five girls was in time so they were able to enroll in Wichita University. During their imprisonment, they had developed a strong sisterhood that would never be forgotten. When it came to pledging a sorority, they did it all together.

Now all was serene and untroubled in Wichita, Kansas. At least for a while.

———

IT WAS A MONDAY MORNING WHEN DWAYNE AND Donna Sue approached their office. The couple spotted a note on the door. Donna Sue took it and read. "Well! Terry McCarthy wants to see us."

Dwayne pointed. "Aw! That's upstairs."

"It's only one floor, Dwayne."

They walked into the agent's office and were immediately directed to go to Terry in a hurry. The Wheelers knew it was for something very important, since the woman had an expression of alarm on her face.

When they entered, they saw Terry McCarthy and an unknown man. "Hi," McCarthy said. "Take a seat."

The couple settled down to find out what was going on.

"Let me introduce you to Mr. X."

Dwayne snickered. "Is that your first or last name?"

The man snickered back without any genuine humor in the sound. "It's my middle name." He had a briefcase and opened it up. He pulled out a thick folder and opened it, taking out some papers. Mr. X looked over at Dwayne. "You received a Government Convenience Discharge over in Germany in 1946."

Dwayne shrugged. "And I deserved it. After all, I was—"

"—fooling around in the black market," Mr. X said, finishing Dwayne's statement.

"Yeah," Dwayne said. "And when I came back to

Wichita, I couldn't get on the police force because I didn't have an Honorable Discharge. So I settled for a private detective license."

"You were angry, right?" Mr. X asked.

"At that time, I was, but now I realize I deserved what I got."

"That's good, Dwayne."

Mr. X closed the folder and pulled out another sheet of paper. He smiled at Donna Sue. "You must be angry at the Boeing Airplane Company for them firing you and the other women when the war was over."

"Of course," Donna said. "That's because the people fired were all the women. Even the stupidest men were kept on."

"I guess you're still mad at them, right?"

"Yes, I am!"

He looked at Dwayne. "But you're not exactly angry with the US Army, are you?"

"I told you I deserved what I got."

"Do you suppose that you could act like you were mad as hell at the Army as Donna Sue is angry at Boeing?"

"What's this all about?"

"What do you think of Communists?" Mr. X asked.

"You mean Commie Russians?"

"That's exactly who I mean."

"I don't like 'em. When I was in Germany, the Soviet Army was harassing the Americans, English, and French all the time. They would block intersections, close up shops and other crap like that."

"Well, would you like to get even with 'em?" Mr. X asked.

"I guess so."

Mr. X looked at Donna Sue. "How about you? Are you mad at Boeing to get even?"

"Oh, well," Donna Sue said with a sigh. "I guess not. I'll let bygones be bygones."

Mr. X asked, "Do you mean that?"

Donna Sue thought a moment, "No! I hate 'em!"

Dwayne was confused. "What's this all about? What is your real name?"

"I'll tell you when the time is right."

"Okay...Mr. X."

Donna Sue wasn't sure about what was going on. "I don't like this secret stuff."

"Would you do it if it would make you a good American?"

"Certainly."

"Then you'll be glad you took part in it," Mr. X stated. He started to put away the papers in the briefcase. "I'll get back to you."

CHAPTER 30

The next time Dwayne and Donna Sue were met by Mr. X, it was in their office. The mysterious man had some more questions.

"Do you know Oskar Hanson?"

"Barely," Donna Sue said. "His daughter was kidnapped and taken to Mexico. We both took part in getting her and four other girls back to Wichita."

"What's this Boeing scientist stuff?" Dwayne wanted to know.

"You'll find out," Mr. X said. "If you are still willing to take part in something patriotic."

Dwayne and Donna Sue glanced at each other, then she said, "Yes."

Mr. X actually grinned. "You two will soon find out."

———

DWAYNE AND DONNA SUE, WITH PACKED suitcases, were picked up at their apartment by Mr. X.

"Listen," Dwayne said. "Where in the hell are we going?"

"As of now, I'm taking you to McConnell Air Force Base. From there, you'll be on your way to your destination."

The couple sat in the back seat, staying quiet. When the car went through the gate, they looked out the windows. Mr. X drove over to a Beechcraft airplane and stopped.

He got out and opened the door for them. "Okay. I'm proud of you guys."

A young airman picked up their suitcases and took them into the airplane, Dwayne and Donna Sue followed. The pilot and copilot were in the cockpit.

The young airman was friendly. "We've got a lot of snacks and soft drinks. Just shake a finger at me, and it'll be 'you call, I haul.'"

The engines were started, seat belts fastened, and within five minutes, the aircraft was going down the runway, then it went airborne.

Dwayne frowned. "Hey, Donna Sue, did we ask where we were going?"

"Not really. All he said was something about a destination."

"I guess we'll find out when we get there."

———

THE BEECHCRAFT HAD EXTRA GAS TANKS AND stayed in the air for what seemed long hours to the two passengers. The couple had three snacks. Dwayne asked the young airman if there was any Orange Crush.

"No, sir. All we've got is Coke and root beer. Sorry."

"That's all right," Dwayne said mournfully.

He and Donna Sue slept between the snacks.

———

THE PITCH OF THE ENGINE INDICATED A slowdown. Then the loud squeaking of the flaps indicated a quick, controlled landing.

Dwayne and Donna Sue glanced out their window and noted a reddish sun was easing up out of the east.

The Beechcraft came to a stop. The airman picked up their suitcases and went down the steps of the aircraft. Dwayne tried to tip the youngster, but he politely refused the gesture.

A 1942 government Chevrolet Sedan rolled up and came to a stop. A figure got out of the back seat and walked toward them. Dwayne and Donna Sue were stunned and surprised.

"Hey, you guys!" Pete Van Dyke said.

CHAPTER 31

The chauffeur drove the car from the airport with Pete Van Dyke in the front seat while Dwayne and Donna Sue were in the back. Pete was a former Army officer who had served with Dwayne in Germany. They had been mixed up together in the black market there, but Dwayne was the one who had gotten caught. He had never held that against Pete, and since the war, they had worked together on several deals, some of them legal, most of them not so much.

"I'm sorry about having to ride in this car, but it belongs to the US government," Pete said, turning around to look at his best friends. "And we're not staying in a fancy hotel. It's a farmhouse which is a safe house. It's in the Virginia countryside."

The driver sniggered. "He's been complaining since he got here two days ago."

Pete smirked back. "Let me introduce you to Harry Baxter, a government employee. I am a man of means, but he doesn't understand that."

Donna Sue spoke to Pete. "Does that mean Sybil won't be with you?"

"My wife is with me and looking forward to seeing you again," Pete said.

"What are we gonna do and why?" Dwayne asked.

"I'm not sure myself."

———

Harry Baxter turned off the highway and went through a small town. From there, he kept going until he reached a place with a few houses, a filling station, and a small diner. After passing through it for a half mile, he turned onto a dirt road.

"Okay," Pete said. "Now we got three miles of bumps."

Fifteen minutes later, they came to a gate. Harry pulled up and reached out of the window to push a card in a slot. The barrier swung open automatically, and Harry pressed on the accelerator and drove over to the dwelling.

The house was two stories high, a large and expansive structure that looked like it had been built many years ago but built to last. Pete got out and opened the door to let Dwayne and Donna Sue out. Harry went to the trunk and set Dwayne and Donna Sue's suitcases on the ground.

"C'mon," Pete said. "He'll want a tip."

Harry laughed. "Pete, I'll bet you haven't given a waiter, a redcap or a shoe shiner any more than twenty-five cents when you tipped 'em."

"My god!" Pete said. "I never tip more'n a dime!"

Dwayne and Donna Sue laughed as Harry drove off to put the car away.

Pete led them through double doors that opened up

on a lush front room with comfortable furniture. "Come on. Your living space is upstairs. They said to put you into room fifteen down the hall. I have the key."

Dwayne and Donna Sue entered and saw comfortable lodgings that included a living room with two lounger chairs, two sofas, and a sideboard. A counter was on the other side that held a coffee maker, coffee cups, glasses, and liquor to drink from them. A small refrigerator was next to that arrangement.

The bedroom had a king-size bed with bedstands on each side. There was also a dresser and chest of drawers. A door opened onto the bathroom with bath and shower, sink and toilet. All new and in perfect condition.

Pete lit a Pall Mall cigarette. "There's a dining room and kitchen downstairs for meals. Would you like to see more?"

"Damn, Pete! This place is fancier than our apartment in Wichita."

"I want to go see Sybil," Donna Sue said.

"Sure," Pete said. "C'mon. We're three doors down."

Pete and Sybil's quarters were exactly the same as what Dwayne and Donna Sue received. Sybil walked over to Donna Sue and gave her what turned out to be a big hug. Then she gave Dwayne a peck on his cheek.

"I'm so glad to see you two guys!" she said.

"Well, we're glad to see you, too," Donna Sue said. She looked around the room. "This is exactly the same as our lodgings."

"Pete thinks we're camping out in a tent or something."

"Well, dammit! I'd prefer our smaller room in the Riverview Hotel in Wichita," Pete complained. "It had class, not like this glaring hovel."

Sybil changed the subject. "Anybody want a drink?"

"That's another thing," Pete grumbled. "Will you look at this cheap hooch?"

Dwayne grinned. "You can't expect much from the government."

Pete walked over and got four glasses and poured scotch whiskey into them. He passed the liquor around, but Sybil turned hers down. "I'll pass, sweetie. Get me a Coke."

"See what I mean?" Pete said.

They settled down and made small talk until Dwayne and Donna Sue took leave and went back to their rooms to take naps after their trip.

CHAPTER 32

Breakfast the next morning was self-service. The kitchen crew laid out scrambled eggs, bacon, sausage, toast, biscuits, oatmeal, coffee, and cream on a counter.

There were more people seated around the tables than Dwayne and Donna Sue expected. Pete cautioned them not to speak to anyone. Every one of the diners was on some highly secret mission and were not allowed to discuss their assignments, much less have friendly conversations.

When the Wheelers and Van Dykes finished eating, Pete told Dwayne they had fifteen minutes to report to their tactical leader in "D" Room. The two women nodded to their husbands and decided to have another cup of coffee.

"Donna Sue," Sybil said between sips of the brew. "I have to talk to you about a situation. And it's serious."

"Really? What's going on?"

Sybil said, "I'm pregnant."

DWAYNE AND PETE REACHED "D" ROOM AND went in. The place was empty, with a circular table and six chairs.

"Ah hah!" Pete exclaimed as they sat down. "The Knights of the Round Table!"

"Oh god!" Dwayne said, grinning. "I hope we don't have to joust. My horse isn't feeling well today."

The table had a pitcher of water and four glasses as well as an ashtray at each chair. Suddenly the doorknob clicked and two men walked in.

"Mr. X!" Dwayne exclaimed.

"That's him, all right," Pete said.

Dwayne was also surprised by the second man. "Hello!"

It was Oskar Hanson. The Norwegian showed a friendly smile. "Well, here's my family's hero."

Mr. X was surprised. "He's your family's hero? What did he do?"

"He was one of the rescuers of my daughter and four other young ladies," Oskar said.

Pete and Mr. X were confused. Pete asked. "What the hell was that all about?"

Dwayne said, "Mr. Hanson and I are not free to discuss the matter."

"Okay then," Mr. X said. "First thing, I am *not* Mr. X. My name is Mike Volkonsky. My family immigrated to America from Russia a couple of generations ago."

Cigarettes were lit and strict attention was turned to Volkonsky, who was preparing to begin the conference.

DONNA SUE AND SYBIL WALKED INTO THE VAN Dyke rooms. The hostess poured two glasses of wine, then they sat down on the sofa.

"Okay," Donna Sue said. "What's so bad about you being pregnant?"

"Pete will not be pleased," Sybil said. "I'm afraid he'll want me to get an abortion."

"Why would he do that?"

"Pete can get really angry. And I'm afraid a baby would piss him off."

Donna Sue took a sip of wine. "I'm thankful I don't have that same trouble with Dwayne."

"You and Dwayne haven't had any babies," Sybil said. "I've always wondered about that."

The female conversation had begun.

"Well, we have sexual intercourse always without prophylactics since we've had sex," Donna Sue said. "One of us must be sterile, but we haven't bothered to look into it."

"I wasn't a virgin when I married Pete. I had sex with several men before we met and got together. We've been married for a long time, so this baby is Pete's."

"I've been the same way," Donna Sue said. "But if I'm sterile, it could be from working on bombers during the war. There were plenty of chemicals around when we women crawled into small places to weld."

"I suppose," Sybil said. She reached for the bottle. "One of our prophylactics must have failed for me to be pregnant."

"A hole in the rubber, huh?"

"I guess so," Sybil said. She poured them both some wine. "I just hope that Pete doesn't think I've been having sex with other men while he was gone on some faraway operation."

"I think he trusts you, Sybil."

"I don't know. He's gotten real angry with me a few times when I made mistakes or been late...things like that. And when he finds out about the baby, he'll hit the ceiling."

———

MIKE VOLKONSKY PULLED A NOTEBOOK FROM HIS briefcase. "Okay, Dwayne and Pete, from now on, everything I say to you is top secret. When my presentation is finished, then Oskar will take over." He grew even more serious. "Are you ready?"

"Let's get to it," Pete said irritably.

Volkonsky began. "The Soviet Union has become a thorn in the side of the west. Those Commies have grabbed up Hungary, Poland, East Germany, etcetera. They need to get a big kick in their asses that would scare and confused them." He glanced at Dwayne and Pete. "You two gentlemen will be contacting two Russian NKVD agents with a blueprint of a secret aerial machine weapon. When you pass that information to them, they will present you with twenty-five thousand United States dollars. At that point—"

"—just a goddamn minute," Pete growled. "What's to keep those bills from being counterfeit?"

"I'm glad you brought that up, Pete," Volkonsky said. "There is an unwritten agreement between American traitors and the NKVD not to play tricks on each other."

Dwayne was worried, and he gave Volkonsky a hard look. "How do you know all about this tricky stuff?"

"Would I be a traitor if I was making this presentation?"

"Well, what about this gift of a secret machine?"

Pete was getting worried. "You're a Russian, aren't you?"

Volkonsky lost his temper. "Listen up, you two! I know you're rootin' tootin' guys who made a combat jump with the Argentine Army, but I know what I'm doing when I take on a case!"

Dwayne was surprised. "How did you know about that parachute jump?"

Volkonsky glared at him.

Dwayne was chastised. "Sorry."

"Me too," Pete said.

Volkonsky turned to Oskar. "I'll turn this over to Oskar's place in the operation."

Oskar began. "I have a lot of experience on aerial instruments like compass bearings, bombsights and weaponry," Oskar said. "I created the blueprints of a combination of those sorts of instruments working together. They can be installed in an airplane in which one pilot can do aerial warfare accurately and quickly. I call the machine the L.A.B., i.e., the *Lightning Attack Bomber*."

"Wow!" Dwayne said, very interested.

"Yes," Oskar said. "At first I was working on the blueprint in Norway. I wanted to pass it over to the Germans to crash their Stuka dive bombers. But before I could finish the blueprint, the Norwegian underground rescued my family and me. I ended up in Wichita working at Boeing. Thus, I had no use for the plans." He paused and lit up a cigar. "Now there is a certain small bomber in the Soviet Air Force that could readily fly and fight with that L.A.B."

Dwayne was confused. "Why do you want to send the blueprints to those damn Russkies?"

"If the Russians install the L.A.B., they will fly them

until a connection between the compass bearing and bombsight will switch off. When that happens, the entire machine will freeze up and the airplane will stall and... well...I hope the pilots have parachutes."

Dwayne and Pete exchanged grins.

"And now," Volkonsky said. "You two are going to act as turncoats and meet with the NKVD agents and turn over the blueprints. And the Communists will hand over a cool twenty-five thousand dollars to you guys."

Dwayne was now curious. "Why did you pick me and Pete for the job?"

Volkonsky said, "I made a check on both of you. You had a bad discharge from the Army and Pete dealt in stolen wealthy art. And I wouldn't be surprised if he worked on the black market with you. I got the NKVD to think of you as criminals who are ready to work for the U.S.S.R."

Dwayne and Pete both shrugged, not denying the things Volkonsky had said about them.

"Where and when are we going to pull this off?" Pete wanted to know.

"Next Wednesday," Volkonsky answered. "You two will meet the two NKVD agents at one a.m. in Virginia Pine Park between here and Washington, DC"

CHAPTER 33

A serious meeting was going on in the Soviet Union Embassy in Washington, DC Grigori Gorchakov and Nikolai Chernishev were seated on the other side of the Attaché Josef Miskov's desk.

Miskov, a colonel in the Soviet Union Air Force, briefed the agents. "You'll go to your usual contact point in Virginia Pine Park a week from this coming Friday at one a.m. This is a very important exchange."

"Will Volkonsky pass the material?" Chernishev asked.

"No," Miskov said. "There'll be two men...American Communists...to meet with you. Any questions?"

Gorchakov shook his head. "Is the password still the same?"

"Right," Miskov answered.

"Then, as the Americans say, it will be a piece of cake."

PETE AND SYBIL VAN DYKE WERE GETTING READY for bed. Sybil was looking at a *Life Magazine*, really not reading it. She could hear Pete brushing his teeth.

When he finished, he came out of the bathroom and slid into his side of the bed. He noticed her reading. "Any interesting in *Life*?"

Sybil sighed and cleared her throat. "Pete?"

"Yeah?"

She took a deep breath. "I'm pregnant."

Pete looked over at her. "What?"

"I'm pregnant."

"You're kidding, right, Sybil?"

"No."

Pete looked at her in surprise. "Pregnant? My god! Pregnant?"

Sybil didn't say anything.

"Oh, Sybil! That's wonderful! Wonderful! How long have you known?"

Sybil looked closely at him. "Two weeks."

"Sybil, darling, I am giddy! Happy! Joyful!"

She smiled. "I thought you might be angry about it."

"How can you say that?"

"I guess I was kind of bashful about it."

"Hey! We *are* married, ya know?" He leaned over and kissed her. "By the way, if it's a boy, let's name him Dwayne, and if it's a girl, let's name her Donna Sue."

"I'd like that, Pete."

"Yeah!" He sunk into five full minutes of happy thoughts before speaking again. "You know what? I'm gonna stop with this adventurous stuff. We're millionaires! I think we should go over to the Hamptons on Long Island to live out our lives. There're some really grand mansions there."

Sybil burst into tears of joy. "Yes...yes...yes! Let's do that, Pete!"

"Okay. And this operation here will be my last."

———

DWAYNE WHEELER DROVE THE '36 CHEVROLET with Pete Van Dyke at his side. They were on the narrow road that led through Virginia Pine Park.

"I think we're getting close," Pete said.

"Look!" Dwayne said. He saw a gnarled tree in the illumination of the headlights and quickly stopped. He turned off the engine while Pete pulled up the envelope with the blueprints inside.

A couple of men appeared from the trees. They walked over and the man in the lead said, "Forty-Three."

"Thirty-Two," Pete replied to get up to Seventy-Five. He reached down on the floorboard and pulled up the packet holding the blueprints. He handed it over, saying, "Hooray for Josef Stalin!"

The man was startled, then he answered. "Yes. Hooray for Comrade Josef Stalin."

———

A WEEK PASSED, AND THE BLUEPRINTS MADE BY Oskar Hanson had been passed through the Kremlin's Air Ministry. Air Marshal Petr Arakansky found it acceptable, and he had his adjutant drive the plans from Moscow over to the Lenin Air Academy.

This was a school, training field, and scientific location. The blueprint, named *BISTRIE ORLITSA,* i.e., SWIFT EAGLE, by the Soviet Air Force, was handed over for technicians to begin making the instrument. The committee decided the aircraft MiG-5 designed by Comrade Mikoyan Gurevich would be suited for what the blueprint offered.

The combination of compass bearing, bombsights, and machine gun weaponry was built and a MiG-5 was rolled out with the Swift Eagle installed. A test pilot, Senior Lieutenant Aleksei Sperev, was chosen to fly the first trial.

The eager young officer took off from the Lenin Air Academy and flew over to a gunnery area and made several runs strafing and bombing targets. When he returned to the Academy, he reported that the Swift Eagle was the best armament he had ever flown.

A squadron of MiG-5s was quickly equipped with the Swift Eagle to serve Mother Russia's enemies in the West.

————

THE RESULTS OF THE EXPERIMENTS WERE SENT to Comrade Josef Stalin, the Generalissimo of the Soviet Union. Stalin was overcome with joy. He invited Air Marshal Petr Arakansky, Colonel Josef Misgov, Senior Lieutenant Aleksei Sperev, Grigori Gorchakov, and Nikolai Chernyshev to visit him in the Kremlin.

He awarded them with Russia's highest medal of *heroism of the Soviet Union.*

CHAPTER 34

Pete and Sybil Van Dyke invited Dwayne and Donna Sue Wheeler to accompany them on their mansion hunting in the Hamptons. They wanted something on the East End of Long Island.

The Van Dykes found what they wanted in the hamlet of Northport. It was a place of beautiful villages with a historic farming community background. The mansion was a huge house with a swimming pool, garden, tennis court, multi-car garages, and stables.

Dwayne and Donna Sue turned down an invitation to stay for a while. They were feeling smothered by such opulent surroundings.

Wichita, Kansas, was calling them.

SEVERAL CAPERS WERE WAITING FOR DWAYNE and Donna Sue. Dwayne acted as a bodyguard for a man who was caught with another man's wife; served as a night lookout for a used car lot; cleared up some shoplifting in a downtown department store; guarded the inventory of a jewelry store that was being moved to another location; and watched over a clothes factory in the warehouse neighborhood.

It took eight months for Dwayne to do all that. Both he and Donna Sue were tired, so they decided to go for a two-week motoring vacation.

———

THE *BISTRIE ORLITSA*, I.E., SWIFT EAGLE, suddenly came apart during an aerial demonstration. It had been upgraded to be operational in a bomber regiment when suddenly everything stopped working. The planes plunged to the earth and exploded in fiery crashes. It was a costly failure.

Comrade Josef Stalin was livid with rage.

Petr Arakansky, Josef Misgov, Aleksei Sperev, Grigori Gorchakov, and Nikolai Chernyshev were stripped of the *Hero of the Soviet Union* medals and were handed shovels to be used in Siberian coal mines.

And Josef Stalin swore vengeance on those who had humiliated him. Somehow, and he vowed that he would find out how those damned Americans had to be behind it...

———

DWAYNE AND DONNA SUE GOT BACK FROM THEIR trip and were fresh and ready to jump back into caperville. With a big grin on his face, Dwayne stood in the office, rubbed his hands together in anticipation, and said, "Let's solve some crimes!"

IF YOU LIKE THIS, YOU MAY ALSO ENJOY: THE FINGER TRAP

TONY FLANER BOOK ONE BY JOHNNY WORTHEN

When half measures don't get you the whole truth...

Tony Flaner is a part-time comedian and full-time commitment-phobe who has never been able to stick with anything in his life. After his fourteen-year marriage ends in divorce, Tony's life takes a dramatic turn when a drunken party ends in murder.

With his life on the line, he must uncover the identity of the mysterious girl who was murdered and how they ended up together in the first place. This undertaking is not just about clearing his name—Tony needs to prove to himself and everyone else that he can finish something for _once in his life_.

But when Tony discovers that his fate is intertwined with that of the mysterious girl he hardly knew—and that their lives are connected like a Chinese finger trap—he unknowingly embarks on a journey full of twists and turns around every corner.

Can Tony Flaner finish this one task and clear his name before he gets sent to prison for a murder he didn't commit?

AVAILABLE AUGUST 2023

ABOUT THE AUTHOR

Patrick Andrews was born an Army Brat on January 14, 1936—his sister's arrival just two years later. His father was a paratrooper in the 82nd Airborne Division during World War II. His mother was a good army officer's wife, who, like several of her lady cousins, wrote short-stories and poems.

After the war, Patrick's father transferred into the Army Reserves, and they moved to Wichita, Kansas—where Patrick caught the scribbling bug. When Patrick got a job as a copy boy at the *Wichita Eagle* newspaper, he was ecstatic.

A few years later, Patrick got a yen to be a paratrooper. He enlisted in the Army and took basic training in Camp Chaffee, Arkansas, soon after being transferred to the 82nd Airborne Division in Fort Bragg. His career with the 82nd was rewarding—being promoted to sergeant and tasked with training cadets in West Point before retiring.

When Patrick read James Jones' *From Here to Eternity*, he appreciated the pride and struggling of soldiers. Soon after, he moved to San Diego, California and began writing and mailing manuscripts while working at a union typesetting company. He married and had one child, named William Patrick.

One pivotal night, Patrick was with a couple of his writing buddies, drinking scotch whiskey and playing at writing the *Sixgun Samurai* series. The next day, they drove up to Pinnacle Books in Los Angeles, where they walked out with a book deal. Patrick and his friends went on to write the series' twelve novels—which were also printed in the U.K. by Star Books, the paperback division of W.H. Allen & Co.

From then on, Patrick started writing and selling western, men's adventure, and military fiction. Years passed, and he had 24 published e-books with Piccadilly Publishing in the U.K.

Today, all six of Patrick's Wichita Detective books are getting another chance to see the light of day—with Rough Edges Press—and find refuge on a cozy shelf in Ocean Hills, California where Patrick and his beloved wife, Julie, live.